UNDER TWILIGHT
Fearless Destiny Series

Debbie Cassidy

1

How long had I been queen? Oh yes, barely three hours and already the mantle of responsibility was beginning to sit heavy on my shoulders. I looked down at the woman kneeling at my feet—a maid I'd seen about the palace when I'd been here for the Black Moon Ball. Her body trembled with fear, and her eyes were dinner plates in her head. The chamber was empty except for two guards, Davin, and the maid. "A closed judging," Davin had said. Why had I come back from my flight around the kingdom early? I could have been enjoying the sweet air and five more carefree minutes. But Erebus had been waiting for me—was still waiting for me. Telling him I'd withheld the location of his lost brethren was going to suck. This judging would probably be an excellent warm up to that conversation.

Resting my elbow on the arm of my magnificent throne of iron and bone, I leaned toward Davin. "What is she accused of, again?"

He kept his eyes on the woman. "Treason, your majesty. All employees and guests of the crown are being searched to ensure Lord Kai left no spies, and we found a cipher in her chambers."

"She works for Kai?"

Davin shook his head. "No. We found assassins ink."

"Assassins ink?"

"It is invisible until viewed under a twilight moon."

"As in the moon in Twilight? You think she works for Twilight?"

"Yes."

The woman shook her head, her eyes wide. "Please, majesty. I implore thee. Please have mercy."

Well that would explain how Orin had known to attack Baal and me when we'd left the Black Moon ceremony. But it was hard to believe that this timid, frightened creature was a spy. She couldn't be more than sixteen or seventeen years old.

I leaned forward. "What's your name?"

"Ella, your majesty."

"Ella, are you a spy?"

She pressed her lips together, her eyes brimming with tears, and then burst into loud body-shaking sobs.

Oh great. I pulled a handkerchief from my pocket and passed it to Davin. He took it gingerly, as if unsure what I meant him to do with it. I jerked my head toward the inconsolable female. His expression cleared, and was that a glint of surprise in his bright eyes? He stepped off the podium next to me and walked over to the maid. Placing a hand on her shoulder to get her attention, he handed her the handkerchief.

She looked up, her eyes red and raw from crying. She mopped at her face and took several shuddering breaths to compose herself. When she spoke, her voice was thick and raspy.

"They had my parents. They had them and they threatened to kill them if I didn't ... didn't do what they wanted."

"The Twilight King?"

She nodded. "A few months ago I received a note, along with my parent's engraved wedding rings. It said that my parents were now Orin's guests, and if I wished them to live I must do as instructed. The package of ink arrived the next day. I was told to write my observations and place them into the maze once a week at midnight."

So, someone else was picking up the notes. More spies. Damn, this place was probably teaming with them—Kai's and Orin's and goodness knew who else's. The throne had been open for conquest for far too long, and although Kai had unofficially claimed the kingdom, I was sure others had also had their eye on it. Hoped and plotted for the chance to slip in and stage a coup of some sort. But now I was here, the rightful heir, and they could all sod off.

"Do you have the note you were sent?" Davin asked the girl.

She shook her head, eyes wide. "I was instructed to burn it."

If I were a sceptical person, I'd wonder at the convenience of that statement, but there was something about the girl, a sincerity that tugged at my heart strings. I wanted her to be a victim, because if she wasn't, then I'd have to execute her. The possibility brought bile to my throat.

I swallowed the bitter fluid. "Do you have any other proof?"

She nodded. "My parents. They escaped. Or they were helped to escape. They contacted me. I have the letter here." She reached into her apron and pulled out a neatly folded piece of paper.

Davin took it from her and passed it to me. The paper was cheap, the writing scratchy but legible.

Dear daughter, we are safe and we are free. Our liberation came at the hands of a human, can you believe? He and his companions aided us in our escape and now we are making our way to the palace to be reunited with you. We know not what was asked of you in exchange for our survival, but we know it cannot have been anything good. Please be safe and know that you are no longer under duress.

You mother and father.

May we meet soon.

A human had saved them. Could they be talking about Brett? He'd been held prisoner. Her story rang true, my gut screamed it.

"Your majesty?" Davin asked.

Dammit if I didn't believe the girl. She was no calculating spy, she was just a scared girl trying to save her parents' lives. "Take her to her chambers and post a guard outside her door. Speak to her parents once they arrive and confirm her story. I trust your decision."

He inclined his head. "As you wish."

The girl swayed and fell to her knees. "Your majesty, you are most gracious."

Game-face time. Composing my features and injecting a hard edge to my stare, I pinned her to the spot with my gaze. "If your story is true then you have nothing to fear."

She nodded earnestly, blatantly relieved.

The guards led her from the room and Davin closed the door. "There are more," he said. "We have them in holding cells."

"How many?"

"Nine. Mainly domestic staff."

It figured. Who best to keep watch than the staff that had access to every part of the castle? The maids that cleaned the rooms and turned down the beds, and the kitchen staff that prepared meals and delivered them to the dining room, hovering while the lords and ladies ate and conversed. This palace housed many noble men and women, it was a hub of activity when it came to politics, or at least it had been. Nine spies could be nine executions—a great way to begin my reign. You could call it housekeeping. Just do it and move on. But it didn't have to be that way.

I stood up. "Question them, and then let them go."

Davin's brows shot up.

I shrugged. "Look, they either spied under duress like the maid—afraid for their lives or the lives of people they cared about—or they needed the money. Hey, maybe they just hated Kai. It doesn't matter. They may even be new spies sent to watch me. I don't care. Relieve them of their duties, but let them keep their lives. I will not have their blood on my hands. I'm pretty sure I'll have plenty of that to come soon enough. For now, I'd like to minimise the deaths I'm responsible for."

Davin smiled. "Kai would have had them executed in a heartbeat. But he'd have tortured them first."

"Yeah, well Kai's an arsehole."

Davin snorted. "Yes. That he is."

Almost at the door, I faltered. Here I was giving orders as if he was my lackey. "Are you okay to deal with this? You don't have to."

"I said I wished to stay and serve you, and I meant it. It would be my honour."

"Thanks. But let me know if I get too bossy, 'kay?"

He chuckled. "Oh, you can count on that."

I left him to his task and headed out to the gardens. Erebus was waiting, and my stomach quivered because I was about to drop a bombshell on him.

***

The dark djinn was strolling through the flowers, stopping here and there to smell what looked like roses. I bit back a smile. Erebus smelling the roses, ha, who would have thought the man had time for such simple pleasures? But then there was too much I didn't know about him. It was strange seeing him outside of Evernight. His leather-bound body was at odds with the vibrant colours of the garden, the leather vest, more body armour than clothing. He had on his classic loose pants that allowed free movement, and sturdy boots suitable for the harsh terrain of Evernight. But he hadn't always lived in the darkness. This had been his home once. He'd grown up here, within these walls, probably played in this very garden as a child. A child ... It was impossible to imagine him as something small and fragile. Erebus was a force of nature, and even several feet away his presence had a tangible impact on my pulse and my heartbeat—excitement, and apprehension, and yes, a smidgen of fear. He paused in his appreciation of the blooms, the muscles of his bare shoulders tensing. Yep, he sensed my presence.

"Did you enjoy your flight?" He asked. He turned slowly to face me and his gaze raked me from head to toe. "Ibris's colours suit you."

I looked down at my outfit—crimson and gold—the colours of my house. "Thank you." I glanced up at the sky. "You saw?"

He blinked slowly. "Your 'whoops' of exhilaration were audible to many."

Ah, yeah. Of course. Brushing back tendrils of hair, I walked over to a nearby bench. "Sit, please."

He took me up on my offer, and I realised how relatively small the bench was in comparison to his powerful frame.

"You wished to see me?" he asked.

"Yes." Oh boy, how to phrase this. Best just come out and say it. "I know where your people are."

He stared at me blankly for a long beat with his silver eyes.

Had he heard me? He'd gone so still, like a predator about to pounce. I licked my lips nervously. "I know where the dark djinn are."

And then what I'd just said must have registered fully, because his eyes flared and narrowed. "You know where they are? How?" His chest rose and fell erratically, and he reached for me, fingers digging into my shoulders. "Is this some kind of joke?"

A growl ripped through the air and Erebus was torn off me. Fargol planted himself between us. Where the heck had he come from?

"No one hurt Kenna. Fargol hurt you bad." The gargoyle flexed his huge hands as if eager to follow through on the threat.

Erebus picked himself up off the ground, his eyes wide with shock. "Fargol," he held up his hand. "I mean her no harm."

"It's okay Fargol. I just gave Erebus some news that shocked him."

"Shock not mean he hurt you."

I placed a hand on the stone man's back. "It's all right. I promise."

He turned his massive head to look down on me. "Fargol stay."

"Yes, that's fine."

Erebus locked gazes with me. His were a burning vortex of confusion and desperation. "Tell me what you know."

I sat down on the bench. "Brett, my best friend, went to Twilight as an emissary for Lindrealm and was held captive. When he escaped he came across an underground chamber where the dark djinn were being held in some kind of stasis. There were black vines twined around them."

His eyes narrowed to slits. "And when did you discover this information."

Guilt stabbed at my chest, but I sat up straight. My decision to delay telling him had been for the greater good. He of all people should understand that. "I knew about it when I came to ask you to increase patrols in Evernight."

He studied me for a long beat and then exhaled through his nose. "You knew I had a right to know immediately, but you wished me to patrol and keep the denizens out of Orin's clutches."

"Yes."

"I understand why you did it. I know withholding that information must have been hard for you."

His white knuckled hands told me this news was hard on him too. Erebus was a man of action, and knowing that the location of his people had been known for some time and nothing had been done to retrieve them was probably killing him.

His lips curled in a hard smile. "You will make a good queen Kenna. Being a monarch comes with its fair share of difficult decisions."

"So you're not mad?"

His top lip curled. "Oh, I'm mad all right. Just, not with you."

"Orin."

"Yes." He stood and inclined his head. "With your permission I would like to leave to liberate my people." His smile was brittle and laced with vengeance. "Once we have my people back we will finally have the numbers to defend both the fifth dimension and Lindrealm. And Orin will know the true wrath of the djinn."

Something had been bugging me for a while, ever since I'd discovered that the dark djinn were being held by Orin, but so much had been happening there'd been no time to dwell, until now. "It's obvious that Orin took the dark djinn in order to weaken Ibris, I mean, they are uber-warriors, right?"

He nodded slowly. "They fought in Ibris's name on many occasions."

"And Orin probably used The Hunt to capture them. It explains why they were unable to fight back effectively. I get all that, but why wait till now to make his move? Why wait all this time?"

Erebus began to pace. "The dark djinn vanished after the first alliance wars. Ibris found me, untouched and unclaimed, and took me in. And then a mere twenty-five years later we were hit with the second alliance wars. It came out of nowhere, a sequence of misunderstandings between lords. But maybe … maybe the misunderstandings were planted?"

"By Orin?"

"Yes. If not for Baal's intervention and his acts of diplomacy, the war would have stretched for decades. But Baal arranged a sit down with all the lords, and the alliance wars ground to a halt before too much blood could be shed."

Yes, that sounded like Baal—the peacemaker. Words were his weapon of choice. "So Orin lost his chance then."

"Yes, and not long after that Ibris was killed." He inhaled sharply.

The horrific connection occurred to me too. Oh god. "You don't think?"

"It's possible Orin may have orchestrated the massacre." His eyes were ablaze with rage. "Removing Ibris from the equation left us bereft and broken. The alliances dissolved, but instead of war there was dissention."

"And the hoard was born." It made sense. "The hoard stopped him. It put a spanner in the works. It was something he hadn't anticipated, an obstacle he wasn't sure how to scale."

"And so he waited and bided his time."

"Until I pushed back the hoard." Oh fuck.

Erebus ran a hand over his face. "The hoard, the largest threat to Lindrealm, was our biggest defence."

I shook my head. "I'm sorry."

"No, don't be. The only person who will be sorry is Orin. He will pay for what he's done. We will stop him. I must go prepare to liberate my brethren."

"Who will you take with you?"

"I need no one."

"Baron, Vale, and Aiden?"

"No, they are patrolling Evernight to protect the denizens from abduction at Orin's hands. We cannot allow him to make more mutations to add to his army. We have, so far, captured and tortured two of Orin's lackey's. Neither uttered a word to deny or confirm their master's identity, and yet they were both Twilighters."

He was planning to go into enemy territory alone. My chest fluttered with anxiety. I couldn't allow him to do this solo. "I'm coming with you."

He blinked down at me, his mouth parting in surprise, and then his expression smoothed out. "No."

The flutter morphed into a stab of annoyance. I arched a brow. "I wasn't asking for your permission. I'm your queen. The days of you telling me what to do are over."

He pressed his lips together, probably biting back treasonous curses.

I stood taller. "We'll leave tomorrow night. We won't tell anyone where we're going. Davin rounded up ten spies, one of which worked for Orin. There could be more. We can't take the risk of Orin finding out about our plans or we're fucked. But we won't be going alone."

It was his turn to arch a brow. "We won't?"

I smiled. "You're not the only one with a trusted posse."

2

All right, so they weren't much of a posse but still, Irina and Fargol would be assets. Fargol could act as sentry, and Irina was a bloody battle mage, her magic and fighting skills could come in useful. I'd laid it all out just like that, but Irina was less than impressed with the idea, and the tightness around Erebus's mouth told me he was holding back a few choice words in response to her objections.

He looked Irina over, his expression icy. Irina, to give her credit, didn't even flinch under his frosty regard. She just glared right back, arms folded across her chest.

Fargol sat on my balcony basking in the sunlight. I guess as an employee of the fortress in Evernight he didn't get to see much of the sun. Bless.

"I appreciate how important this is to you, Erebus," Irina said. "And I see how liberating the dark djinn would err in our favour in the war against the Twilight king. But it's a foolish idea. We will be caught. Orin has undoubtedly posted some kind of extra security measures in those tunnels since Brett's escape."

I parked my butt on the edge of my bed, picked up an apple from the bowl of fruit on the side table and took a huge bite. Chewing gave me a moment to think. Irina was a pragmatist. She was looking at the issue as if it were a problem and weighing up the chances of success, which was why she was a good soldier, but this wasn't a conversation to decide whether this mission would happen. That had already been decided.

"Should I regret bringing you in on this, Irina?"

She opened and closed her mouth a couple of times, and then pressed her lips together and shook her head.

"Because we're going, whether you come with us or not. So what is it going to be? In or out?"

"In of course." She huffed. "Baal will not be pleased."

"Who said anything about telling Baal?"

He eyes widened. "You intend to go without informing him?"

"Informing him? Since when did he become my keeper? Last I checked, I was queen. I make my own decisions." The words tasted ashy in my mouth, but I swallowed them and stared steadily at her.

She pressed her lips together. "A wise queen heeds the advice of her counsel."

"By counsel, you mean you?"

She nodded her head. "At present, yes. Baal left me here to help you navigate the complexities of palace life. I admit I wasn't expecting this turn of events, but I would be remiss in my duties if I neglected to tell you that this is suicide."

A frisson of unease skittered up my spine and doubt settled in the pit of my stomach, but one glance at Erebus, and his determined face was enough to melt the anxiety.

"Okay, now we're agreed on going, let's get to the planning part of things." I smiled at Irina, "A plan that minimises the risk of suicide."

Irina snorted.

"There must be a way to get in and get the dark djinn out without being detected. Some magic or spell something that could cloak us? We'll also need something to neutralise the effects of the vine holding the djinn in stasis."

Irina frowned. "I supposed we could cook something up." Her eyes lit up. "This could be just what father needs. A quandary to solve that would benefit the realm and not harm it."

"So, you'll speak to him?"

"Yes."

"How long would it take to cook something up?"

"I don't know. But if I leave now I can be there by nightfall. I'll send word of progress, but it could take days to come up with something."

"Not good enough. We need to leave tomorrow night."

"Why the rush?" she asked.

"The coronation is in two days' time. I intend to use the opportunity to reveal the truth of our predicament and rally the realm to prepare to defend itself against Orin's impending attack. If the dark djinn are free by then, free and at our side, it'd be a huge morale booster."

"It will show them that we can achieve amazing things," Erebus said.

I nodded. "It's a confidence boost they're going to need, because Orin has some serious power on his side. The Hunt and goodness knows how many modified denizens at his command."

Irina paced. "Even if I wanted to get a solution to you by tomorrow night, the journey to my father and back would take a day in itself."

Fargol stretched and stood. "Fargol take Irina. We go now. We come back tonight."

Irina looked from me to Fargol.

I nodded. "Do it."

She walked toward the balcony.

"And Irina?"

She glanced over her shoulder.

"Baal really doesn't need to know. He has enough on his plate right now."

Dark conflict flashed in her eyes, but then she sighed and inclined her head. "As you wish, your majesty."

Ah clever, using my status to quell her loyalty to Baal—after all, allegiance to the sovereign trumped allegiance to your lord, right?

At least I hoped it did.

Fargol rose up into the air, Irina clasped in his epic hands.

And suddenly I was acutely aware that Erebus and I were alone in my bedchamber. He walked out onto the balcony, as if sensing the same thing and wanting to put some distance between us, or maybe it was just me projecting my feelings onto him.

"Do you love him?" Erebus asked.

My heart did a weird flip, partly at the mention of Baal and partly at the smooth rumble of Erebus's voice. "Yes."

"He makes you happy?"

A smile tugged at my lips. "Yes, he does."

Erebus turned to face me, his skin gleaming in the sunlight and his silver eyes squinted against the brightness. "If that ever changes …"

What was he saying?

He stepped into the room blocking out the sunlight, his huge frame dwarfing mine. My lungs tightened and my breath stalled as that familiar concoction of yearning and fear squirmed to life inside me. Adrenaline flooded my system.

His chest was rising and falling rapidly too, and his hands were fists at his side to prevent himself from what? From touching me?

No. I didn't want to know what he wanted. Why did I remember those calloused fingers on my skin? Fuck, this adrenaline needed to go somewhere.

I took a step back. "We should train."

He nodded. "Yes. We may have to fight our way out."

Never mind the fact we'd just decimated hundreds of creatures in the pit. Training it was. Turning on my heel, I led the way out of my chambers. Now where the fuck was the training room in this place?

3

Like silk and steel. He was a wonder to watch. I moved on autopilot, blocking, parrying ducking. His frown turned to a grin of pride as I held my own against him for the first time in forever.

"You've improved," he said.

"It's the new leg." I spun and jabbed.

"No," He jumped back to avoid my strike. "It's you. There is a new confidence."

We sparred for half an hour using wooden swords and he didn't hit me once. Finally, he stepped back and dropped the sword. He held up his hands and beckoned me forward.

"Let's see how good your hand to hand is."

Hand to hand? Against the monolith? It had been a while since I'd done any hand to hand. Quelling the frisson of apprehension, I dropped my training sword and fell into a defensive position.

"When faced with an opponent much larger than you," Erebus said. "The key is to hit then evade. Do not allow your larger stronger opponent to get a grip on you."

Ten minutes of evasion and I was failing. I hadn't managed to get even one hit in, and then I slipped up, ducking too late to avoid a grab. He had me yanked up and pressed against his chest before I realised what was happening. I squirmed, desperate to free myself, my back rubbing up against his leather-bound torso. He flipped me around, lifted me up, and slammed me against the mats before covering me with his body, pinning me down.

"Fuck. Fine you made your point." I stared up at the ceiling, blinking to clear the dots in my vision.

His face appeared above me, feral and concerned. "Did I hurt you?"

"You just slammed me into the mat, what do you think?"

His inner thighs were pressed up against my outer thighs, his hands pinning my wrists to the mat above my head. A wave of déjà vu washed over me. We'd done this before at the fortress. He'd been a mentor to me then, luring me out of the darkness of my disability. We stared at each other now, just as we had back then, breaths erratic. His silver gaze trailed across my face, dropping to linger on my lips, and there was that visceral tug. Back then I'd have given anything for him to press those lips to mine. But I wasn't that woman anymore. I twisted and bucked, taking him by surprise.

He released me and sat back on his haunches, his expression guarded.

No more hand to hand. "I should go do queen stuff."

He rose to his feet. "I must check in with the others."

"You're going back to Evernight?"

He smiled wryly. "No. I don't need to return to communicate with them."

"One of these days you're gonna have to explain that dynamic to me."

"Maybe."

Leaving him standing in the middle of the room, I headed back to my quarters for a cool bath.

***

The dining room was humming with the conversation of the nobles that had remained at the palace. Djinn servers kept plates filled and goblets topped up with wine. Colourful fabrics were almost an assault on my vision. Usually the hues would lift my spirits, but not today. Today my head was a mess of thoughts and the turmoil clouded the revelry.

From my position at the table on the raised platform above it all, I struggled to put the errant thoughts aside and focus on what Davin was telling me. He'd pointed out who everyone was—educating me in Baal's absence. It was comforting and interesting, but my mind kept drifting to other, more personal, matters.

I loved Baal, but I was about to go on a mission without telling him. He was in my heart, rooted deep and comfortable. His smile, his laughter, his wicked sense of humour and that look in his eyes just before he kissed me. My pulse kicked up at the memory. So what the fuck was this shit with Erebus? Why was I feeling this way?

Davin poured me some more wine. "You look troubled."

"It's nothing." I picked at the sleeve of my crimson and gold tunic. It was either this or one of the overly corseted affairs most of the ladies were wearing. There was already way too much bosom on display without me adding mine to the equation.

His gaze grew intense. "If it troubles you then it is something. May I hazard a guess as to your quandary?"

I sat back, lips twitching; this should be good. "Sure. Go ahead. Hazard your guess."

"You're confused about your feelings toward Erebus."

Well fuck me sideways. "How the heck?"

He shrugged. "I have exceptional perception skills."

I gulped my wine. "It doesn't mean anything."

Davin smiled. "We are complicated creatures, your majesty, and our hearts and minds aren't always in accordance with each other, sometimes out bodies take the reins."

"Look, please call me Kenna when we're not doing the formal audience stuff. And what are you trying to say? That I have no control over my sexual urges?"

"Of course not. I'm saying it is possible to want two people at the same time."

"Urgh, No. Not for me it isn't. I love Baal."

"Yes I believe you do."

"It's just, when I'm with Erebus there's this excitement, this heat, the kind you usually only experience when you're fighting for your life."

"And this exhilarates you?"

"Yes."

Davin smiled. "You are Ibris's spawn, a warrior at heart just like your sister Dante. Erebus and Dante were the best of friends. They fought side by side. They trained together, they were inseparable. And then she fell in love with Baal."

Well this was news. "How do you know this?"

"It's no secret in our realm. Dante and Erebus were a magnificent pair. On the battlefield they were a force to be reckoned with. And there were even rumours that they shared a tent on more than one occasion.

"Shared a tent?"

Davin's brows flicked up.

"Oh." They were fucking. My neck heated at the thought.

He sipped his wine. "They were never officially an item. And Dante's betrothal to Baal was not forced. They were said to be very much in love." He shrugged. "There is a difference between physical attraction and love, although sometimes one can be mistaken for the other."

Yeah, there was definitely an attraction between Erebus and me. But my heart belonged elsewhere. I picked up my fork and jabbed a slice of chicken. What I felt for Baal went deeper than anything I'd felt for anyone before. But Erebus would always have a special place in my heart. I'd been broken when he'd found me, and he'd put me back together. He'd saved me, trained me, and my heart had dared to feel again. But yes, he'd almost broken me with his betrayal, a betrayal I understood now that I had the mantle of monarch on my shoulders.

"Sometimes love and wants and needs just aren't enough. Sometimes the bigger picture is more important."

Davin smiled wryly. "Yes, Kenna. Sometimes it is." His gaze took on a far-off edge.

"So what is your quandary?" I locked gazes with him and he blinked, breaking eye contact.

"Now that is a tale for another day." He smiled amiably. "One far from now when our kingdom is safe."

"Bah! Spoilsport."

He chuckled. "Come, we should mingle with your guests. Let them get to know the queen they will be crowning in two days."

"Am I going to have to wear it?"

"What?"

"The crown? Like all the time?"

He laughed. "No, Kenna. You won't."

"Good. It looks heavy."

Eyes twinkling, he held out his hand and led me onto the floor to meet my public. Time to smile and be gracious, when all I really wanted to do was slap an everlight sword in my hand and head out to kill shit. Being a queen was going to take some serious getting used to. Let's hope Baal was having more luck in convincing the Lindrealm government of the threat we were facing.

4

BRETT

A monster stared back at him from the mirror, and the urge to smash the silver surface to smithereens was almost overwhelming. But this face would be the key to convincing the government that they needed to act now, and they needed to act fast.

Orin wasn't playing games, and if Lindrealm was going to survive they'd need to get serious about defensive tactics. Fighting the threat off wasn't even an option. Humanity was sorely outnumbered.

Brett paced the small bathroom, made even smaller due to his increased body mass since his otherworld transformation. Baal had asked him to remain hidden until it was time. They'd entered Baal's office through a mirror portal hidden in a coat closet. And from there Baal had smuggled Brett into the washroom across the hall. The meeting was being held on the top floor of the embassy—the building where all the important decisions were made. Where bills were approved or rejected and where people's lives were changed for better or worse.

He was the pièce de résistance, the cherry on the fucking cake.

And yeah, it made his blood boil and his brain seethe, or was that just how it was gonna be from now on? Was aggression a part of his new DNA?

A rap on the door was followed by Baal's strained face. "Are you ready?"

Brett pulled up his hood. "Yeah," his voice was gravel and glass. "Let's get this over with."

"They've gone over the main itinerary for the meeting," Baal said. "I filled them in on some recent developments, namely Kenna's stay in Evernight and the existence of the hoard. It's about time they knew what was out there, what Erebus has been protecting them from and why they've had to pay the tithe. They need to understand that the djinn are not the enemy."

"And how did they take it?"

"If not for the hoard attack a few weeks back they'd probably have discounted my account."

Why was it that humans played ostrich so easily? Burying their heads in the sand to avoid harsh truths even when the truth slapped them in the face repeatedly? Humans … Was he even human any longer?

Down a corridor they strode, into a lift, way too small to contain them both without physical contact.

But Baal didn't flinch or look away. He held Brett's gaze and smiled.

"Once this is over, I'm sure Kenna would love to see you," he said. "She misses you. And being queen will be a huge adjustment. Having a familiar face about would be soothing."

"This face is far from familiar."

Baal sighed. "I doubt Kenna sees anything but her best friend when she looks at you."

If he had any tears, his eyes would have welled up at that. If only he could see what Kenna saw; instead all he saw was an unyielding diamond body and clear glass eyes. All he could think was there was barely any human left in him.

The lift pinged open on a darkly furnished floor dotted with faux potted plants. The double doors ahead were wide open, and two guards in uniform stood to either side. Brett recognised them as Fearless from central base. Were they using Fearless as security guards now? Didn't they appreciate what they were up against out on the streets? No, probably not. Too busy hiding up here in their cushy meeting room with coffee and sheaves of paper to sign. Fucking decision makers who'd never had to go up against a denizen in their lives. Never lost a loved one to the tithe. Fuckers.

The room was taken up by a horseshoe table, and several men sat around it debating whatever Baal had left them mulling over.

"But we have over fifty new recruits," a guy with salt and pepper hair said.

"Fifty disabled recruits," his heavy-jowled companion reminded him.

"Dammit, if Miss Carter can do the job then—"

"Miss Carter is an exceptional case. And now we know why. Thanks to the chief of the Fearless Programme." The jowly guy inclined his head in Baal's direction.

Baal had revealed Kenna's identity? It looked like shit was getting real then. Brett raised his gloved hand to pull back his hood, but Baal gently tapped his arm in warning. Not yet.

A surge of annoyance bordering on rage climbed up his throat. Pin it down Brett, keep a cool head.

"Gentlemen," Baal said. "Apologies for the adjournment, but I'm ready to continue." He was immaculate in his suit, gems winking at his ears and on his fingers, but that's not what the room saw. To them Baal was an elderly guy with silver hair and a pot belly. Brett knew that persona because he'd met Baal in his avatar many times. The glamour clung to him now, visible to Brett as an amber haze. Why not reveal his true form to them? But then if he did, he may risk losing his foothold on the Fearless, risk losing their confidence. For them to know he was a djinn, that he'd lived among them, deceived them, would be counterproductive right now. The goal was to foster trust. Which was why it was imperative to keep a cool head.

All eyes were on Baal now, and then they were running over Brett's hooded form.

"Who is this?" Salt and Pepper asked.

"This is the Fearless officer who went into Twilight for us."

"Our emissary?"

"Indeed."

"When did he return? Why were we not informed he was back?"

"There were complications," Baal said. "He was held prisoner and experimented on."

The room was suddenly deathly silent until the jowl guy broke it with an incredulous bark of laughter. "Very funny Parsons."

Baal arched a brow. "Minchin, I'm sure you know me well enough to know I do not make jokes."

Minchin swallowed. "Experimented on, you say?"

"Allow me to fill you in." Baal spoke and they listened. He told them of the serum, The Hunt, and the modified denizens. He laid out Orin's plan as plainly as he could, and when he was done there were pale faces all around.

But then the man with the salt and pepper hair snorted. "This is preposterous. Twilight has been nothing but gracious to us since our treaty was signed." He peered at Brett. "It's obvious some offence was caused. Maybe if we'd sent an emissary trained in the art of politics as I'd suggested in the first place …"

The annoyance tipped into fury and Brett yanked back his hood and leapt forward, slamming his hands on the desk. Someone screamed and the eyes on the man before him grew wide as saucers. The smell of urine filled the air and a stab of satisfaction pierced Brett's heart.

"You think this was done because I caused offence?" Brett's tone was a snarl. "The only offence I caused was refusing to sign a treaty that would have delivered us into their hands."

"The document was spelled," Baal added. "A clause we were unable to see. It allowed the emissary full power to sign the treaty—a treaty that would have handed Lindrealm to the Twilight king."

"This is what he wants to do to us." Brett pulled off his hoody to reveal his diamond skin meshed with human flesh. "He wants to turn us into soldiers for his army and march us across Evernight and into the fifth dimension."

Those disgusted expressions were almost too much, but this wasn't about his pride. This was about the greater good, and so he stood still and allowed them to view their fill.

"I was lucky I escaped before the process was complete. I maintained control of my mind, but if he'd finished I'd have been his puppet to control."

The room broke into murmurs.

"They are going to come," Baal said. "The Hunt will storm our lands and they will take our able-bodied men and women and turn them into soldiers for Twilight's army. If we have any hope of stopping them, we need to act now."

"Salt the land around the gates. Salt as much as we can to deter The Hunt," Brett said.

"Salt?" the younger government official asked.

"Yes. It will keep The Hunt at bay."

"What about these modified denizens?"

Brett shook his head. "Mobilise all Fearless and put them on standby. If the enhanced denizens attack, we need to be ready enforce."

"Every Fearless counts," Baal said. "The attack could come at any time. We need to be ready yesterday."

They broke into urgent conversation and Baal handed Brett his hoody. They'd made their point, it was now up to the government to take a stand.

5

Djinn wine did not agree with me. Or maybe it agreed with me too much. How could I have forgotten what it did to me? How it set my body on fire in desperate need to be touched. And Baal was in Lindrealm, too far away to do much of anything. Gah! Sleep, I needed to shut down. The bed seemed empty without Baal's warm hard body to fill it. To fill me. Stop it.

A gentle breeze laced with Baal's scent drifted in off the balcony. Liquorice aroma, heavy and thick, wafted in from the blooms that climbed the wall outside my chambers. Deadly flowers Irina had warned me about. Deadly polyanders.

She'd also said that Baal didn't smell of them, but she was wrong. Or was she? Maybe she couldn't smell him like I could? Yep, that sounded so weird. But then what was going on? Why was this scent in my head every time I was around him? Had it always been there?

No … Not the first time we'd met in the garden in Evernight. I hadn't picked up on it then, no, the first time had been when I'd discovered Erebus's betrayal, when Baal had alerted me to it, just before Erebus and I had …

It was something to ask him about surely. But right now, thank goodness, the wine was wearing off. The fire had melted to a slow burn, turning my limbs liquid and my eyelids heavy. As I hovered in the place between wakefulness and slumber, a phantom weight settled behind me, the mattress dipped, and heat pressed against my bare back. Fingers, calloused and thick, ran down my spine, eliciting a moan and a steady throb at the apex of my thighs.

This wasn't happening, it wasn't real, and yet it was. The connection forged when I'd taken the flame glowed softly between us. The wine had opened the door between us and Erebus was here, not in the flesh but in my mind, his spirit touching mine, the act somehow too intimate.

"Stop." My voice was a trembling whisper.

His breath was a hot caress on the nape of my neck. His hand slipped over my waist and up to cup my breast, aching and tight. My body yearned for him. No. Not him, it cried out to be loved. Baal. I needed Baal. His hand froze, as if sensing my thoughts.

"No." I kicked the door between us closed and collapsed onto my back.

Dammit. No more fucking wine for me.

Grabbing a pillow I shoved it over my head and squeezed my eyes closed. Sleep.

Now.

The sandman obliged, tugging me under. But there was no relief for me there either, as I slipped into someone else's skin.

"Touch me. You know you want to."

"Dante ... please," Erebus's tone was pained.

A sultry laugh. "Please, please, please. What are you afraid of?"

"You know we can't."

A husky sigh, and then the sound of buckles being undone followed by the kiss of air on my skin. "You'd turn this down?"

"Damn you woman."

Hands on my breasts, rough and demanding. A mattress at my back, fingers inside my slick heat. Stroking, stoking, fuck, yes. But more, I needed more.

"Erebus, just fuck me already."

His cock pushing into me inch by inch, filling me, taking me.

"The thrill of the hunt. The pleasure of the flesh."

"Dante, I ..."

"Don't, don't say it. Just show me."

Erebus began to move, and the world shattered.

I sat up, gasping, my body throbbing in the after effects of the most powerful orgasm. Oh shit, I was wet and, shit, wow. What the heck had just happened?

The sound of wings beating the air and a soft thud on the balcony had me scrabbling for my robe.

Fargol was back.

Wrapped in the soft material of my dressing gown, I padded toward the archway.

Irina peered in. "you're awake."

"Um, yeah. Couldn't sleep." Liar liar, vagina on fire.

She held up a leather bag. "I have the solution."

The lingering dregs of the dream dissipated. "Tell me what it does."

Irina parked her butt on the edge of my bed. "We should probably get Erebus in too. I can go through it once and we can formulate a plan of action."

Fargol sat back on his haunches in the arch.

Get Erebus? Like into my bedroom after that … whatever had just happened? "Sure. I'll go find him." After I put some clothes on.

Erebus answered his door, fully dressed and alert.

"You knew I was coming?"

His lips twitched.

Oh shit. Double entendre.

I turned on my heel and strode off toward my chambers. "Irina is waiting."

It had been a dream brought on by what Davin had told me about Erebus and Dante's relationship. Yeah, this was all Dante's fault, and I bet Erebus had sensed … stuff, from the bond we shared. This was so fucked up. Right now, the bond came in useful. With the hoard still active and the gate still needing protecting, I could channel power to Erebus and give him a boost if he needed, or summon him to me if I was in trouble. Yeah. We needed it right now, but once this was all over, that bond had to go.

Irina greeted us with a smile and a tray of tea. When had she had time to make tea? Fargol sat on the floor by the bed, a dainty cup clutched between forefinger and thumb—he looked ridiculous. A snort of laughter exploded from my lips.

Irina rolled her lips between her teeth, her eyes twinkling with mirth.

Fargol sipped his tea, completely oblivious that he was the object of our amusement. Man I loved that gargoyle.

We sat on huge cushions around the low table Irina had prepared, and she poured more tea. "Father was pretty excited about this project. He already had some equations and formulas he'd been playing with for another project which hadn't gone so well, but when I told him what we needed he had an epiphany."

Erebus drained his cup. "What did he create for us?"

Irina set the leather pouch she'd shown me earlier on the table and undid the tie. She carefully extracted a vial.

"It's an invisibility potion," she grinned. "And it works!"

"You tried it?"

"No, father did. He was invisible for almost two hours. And Agares tested it too, albeit reluctantly."

Baal had tasked his general with watching over Caldwell, Irina's father. We couldn't risk him being taken by Orin again. "How is Agares?"

Irina winced. "I think his guard duty is wearing thin. He is eager to be by Baal's side, or here with us at court."

"I'll speak to Baal when he gets back. Maybe we can move your father here too?"

He face lit up. "That would be wonderful. Thank you. But there is more," she glanced at Fargol.

Fargol frowned. "Fargol stay with Kenna."

I looked from the mage to the gargoyle. "What's going on?"

Irina sat forward. "Father is extremely close to finalising the anti-serum, and we were discussing methods of deployment."

"Okay?"

"Father believes he can create bombs that turn into a fine mist upon impact. He suggested we launch them aerially."

"That's an awesome idea."

Fargol made a harrumphing sound.

"You want gargoyles to do it," Erebus said.

"Fargol stay with Kenna," Fargol said firmly.

It was a great plan. If we could get enough gargoyles to carry and launch the bombs, when the denizens did attack we could wipe them out in one fell swoop.

"Fargol?"

He shook his head. "Please do not ask Fargol to leave Kenna."

I sighed. "I wouldn't ask if it wasn't important. Who knows how much time we have before Orin makes his move. We need to be prepared. Can you rally the gargoyles?"

Fargol put down his teacup. "Gargoyles stubborn. It take time to convince them."

Back at the fortress Fargol had needed to feel useful, was that just because he'd been serving the building or was that a gargoyle thing in general? Only one way to find out. "Tell them their queen requests their aid. It would be most helpful"

His eyes lit. "The queen requests aid."

"That's right."

He grinned, showcasing his terrifying teeth. "And if say no, Fargol crush."

"Um, maybe just ask again, nicely?"

He considered this and then shook his huge head. "No. Crushing work much better."

Must be a gargoyle thing. "Fine. You do what you have to and recruit me some gargoyles. I'm counting on you Fargol."

He strode out onto the balcony and stretched his mighty wings. "Fargol not leave Kenna for long." And then he was launching himself into the air.

One part of the bigger plan was in motion. Now to focus on the immediate mission. "Okay Irina, tell me more about this invisibility potion. Do we drink the whole thing?"

She shook her head. "Oh no. Just one drop will render us invisible for an hour. There should be enough here for the dark djinn we're rescuing to use too, if need be. It should help us smuggle them out of the palace."

Yes, this could work. The Twilighters couldn't catch what they couldn't see. It gave us a distinct advantage.

"Thank you Irina. This is fantastic."

She beamed.

"We will have to work fast," Erebus said. "And we have only your friend's oral account of the location."

"Brett was pretty precise, and I had him draw me a map." I retrieved the map from my jewellery box and handed it to Erebus.

He studied it for a long moment. "This is surprisingly detailed."

"Yeah, Brett has exceptional observation skills."

Erebus laid the map on the table and traced the weave of the river with his finger. "We can enter Twilight through the Black Forest here, cross the river here, and access the palace catacombs here. From there, as long as we don't draw attention to ourselves, we should be able to break into the chamber my people are being held in from below, and liberate them."

Irina reached into her pocket and pulled out a dagger. It glinted dully in the lamplight. "Iron," she said. "You said the djinn were being held in slumber by some kind of vine? I did some research, and there is only one vine that can do that. It's called the obsidian narcos, and it can be poisoned with iron."

So we had all we needed. We had the potion, the dagger, and a map. "We leave at dusk." I stood and brushed down my slacks. "Get some rest everyone. We're going to need our strength."

6

"You're going to do what?" Davin stared at me in horror.

"I'll be fine. I just need you to keep things ticking while I'm gone." I adjusted my jacket, the softest black leather. It fit like a glove and was super easy to move in. The royal tailor had even made me soft leather slacks that weren't too tight on my legs to allow for my prosthetic. The man was a genius, and he worked insanely fast.

"Kenna! You're a monarch. You can't just go swanning off into danger. You have people to do that for you."

"What kind of monarch would I be if I sat back and let others do all the dirty work? I need to lead by example."

Davin moved around to block my view of the mirror. "Do you think that Ibris ever set foot on the battlefield?"

I blinked up at him. "What? I thought he was brave and fearless and stuff."

Davin's beautiful lips curled in a smile. "No doubt that he was, but he was also the jewel of the realm, and thus was protected. Until death slipped into his home and took him unawares of course. It was the kind of death he could not fight."

"Yes, the poison, the poison that incapacitated him and my family."

Davin inclined his head, and a strand of hair laced with gold and green slipped over his shoulder. I resisted the urge to tuck it behind his ear. He was undeniably beautiful.

"Ibris was an emblem," Davin said. "A powerful figurehead for the realm. But the warriors that kept it safe were a different matter entirely. A monarch protects its people through alliances and political endeavours, and if matters progress to war then he sends an army."

He was right of course, but I wasn't the kind of monarch to sit around drinking tea, twiddling my thumbs and spewing pretty words to make my public love me. I was a woman of action, a woman who led by example. "This isn't war, it's a rescue mission, and to be honest, even if it was a war I'd be on the front lines. Because by staying behind all I'd be doing is sending the message that their lives are worth less than mine."

Why was he looking at me with that odd expression on his face?

"Um, are you okay?"

He nodded. "I will stay behind and watch over the realm for you as you wish. I must make preparations for the coronation." He leaned in and pressed a kiss on my forehead, sudden and firm, then turned on his heel and strode from the room.

My skin tingled where his lips had made contact. What the heck had that been for? But Fargol was landing on my balcony.

It was time to go.

***

"Maybe we should take a carriage?" The huge primal Evernight beast snorted at me—a cross between a horse and a lion, it was jet black, had a tail tipped with spikes, and an armoured head plate. I'd ridden on one once, when we'd galloped through the Evernight to save a settlement from the shadow people. It had been like riding the scariest rollercoaster, except the rollercoaster was alive and could eat you if it wanted.

We were behind the stables, unseen and unheard. The staff had been summoned to an impromptu evening meeting by Davin. He'd spin them a lie about my being away in Lindrealm for diplomatic talks. Enough time for Irina, Fargol, Erebus, and I to exit the palace grounds undetected. An almost full moon hung heavy in the air providing enough light for us see what the heck we were doing.

Irina strapped her pack onto its back—most likely weapons. My everlight sword was tucked in its sheath at my side, although I wasn't sure how effective it would be against Twilighters.

Irina patted one of the ebony beasts. "Beautiful. It's been a long while since I had the pleasure of riding one of these."

Erebus smiled, his eyes lighting up with genuine delight. "You've ridden a leoequise before?"

Irina launched herself up onto the beast's back, her golden braid flicked up behind her, and her tawny eyes glinted in the gloom from her cobalt blue face. "Once or twice." She dropped him a wink. "Question is: can you keep up?"

Erebus let out a burst of surprised laughter and something ugly and unexpected twisted inside me. But then Erebus's hands were closing around my waist, and I was momentarily airborne as he lifted me up onto the fearsome beast. I'd barely taken a breath before he was settling in behind me—too close, too intimate. His large hands gripped the reins and the memory of our last ride surged up to grasp my mind. I'd wanted to touch him back then, and be touched by him. My heart had beat faster in his presence, and there'd been urgency to each breath. But he'd crushed those feelings with his manipulations. Exhaling away the recollection, I flexed my thighs to grip the beasts hide and then we were in motion. Irina took the lead, her beast moving so fast it looked like she was in flight. Erebus let out a whoop and cracked the reins, urging our mount to go faster.

Irina's laugh drifted back to us on the wind and then we were out of the palace grounds and hurtling into the night. We had a hundred miles to go before we hit the forest, and from there we'd continue on foot. The forest spanned the edge of the capital, which touched upon the boundaries of Twilight. The two capitals sat almost side by side, but the Black Forest was a beast in itself, or so Davin had explained. It was a place that would eat you up and spit you out in a heartbeat—filled with the dregs of djinn and Twilight society, creatures that preferred the dark canopy beneath monolithic trees to the sunshine and meadows of their respective worlds.

By Erebus and Irina's calculations, the journey would take a night and most of the next day, but if we timed it right then it would still enter the forest in daylight and emerge at dusk. There was a tavern just over fifty miles from the palace, our first stop for the night.

I raised my voice to be heard above the clatter of hooves and whistle of the wind. "Shouldn't we slow down? Won't the mounts tire?"

Erebus's chest rumbled in laughter. "They'll tire," his breath was warm against the shell of my ear. "But they have several miles in them before slowing down is required."

Irina was still in the lead, but barely by a length. Erebus's thighs flexed behind mine and our mount surged forward, overtaking Irina smoothly.

She laughed again, a sultry sexy sound.

Why was I clenching my teeth?

Long minutes ticked by, and then with a tug on the reins Erebus instructed the mount to slow its pace.

His lips brushed my ear. "You're tense."

Shit, I was. Forcing my body to relax, I leaned into him. "I'm fine. Just anxious about our mission."

He was silent for a long beat. "Ibris had many wives. Do you know why?"

"Um, I assume it's the djinn way?"

He chuckled. "No, it was Ibris's way. Efreet are highly sexed. Ibris was a man with great needs, and to fulfil those needs he needed many wives. Love may have come into it with one or two of them, but for the others it was a purely physical arrangement."

What was he trying to say? My neck heated as suspicion bloomed in my chest.

Erebus's thumb brushed the top of my hand. "You are part efreet, Kenna. Now that you have the flame inside you, you will feel the fire, and you will need to quench it either on the battle field or in the bedroom. But being monarch means the battlefield is forbidden so …"

He was saying I needed to fuck. Yeah, didn't I know it, and as soon as Baal got back I'd get right on that. There was nothing I could do about it now. My dream came back to me, Dante's taunts and Erebus's tortured responses. She'd goaded him into fucking her—used him as a fuck buddy to ease her fire. But he'd wanted her too. It had been evident in the way he'd touched her, the way he'd kissed her. And then she'd fallen for Baal. But it was just a dream, right? My imagination? Wasn't it? But they had been shacking up. Had Erebus been hurt when she'd moved on to Baal? Was that why Erebus had been so easily seduced by another—the woman who'd lured him away from the palace, allowing the slaughter of my family?

"If you need relief, then you may call on me," Erebus said.

Relief? As in sex. Oh god. He was offering himself to me, and for a split second I contemplated it. What the heck was wrong with me?

"I'm fine." I bit out the words.

He chuckled. "If you say so."

He'd felt my need through our bond. Damn. He'd probably felt the aftershocks of my dream orgasm. But there was no denying that he was on to something. My body felt different. It had started when my alters had assimilated, but really kicked into gear once the throne had accepted me. As if something inside me had clicked into place. My true nature had risen to the surface and seeped through my mortal skin, coating it in a sheen of otherworldliness. I was efreet. And if this heightened sex drive was part and parcel of how I was, then it needed to be addressed. But taking multiple lovers was out of the question. My heart belonged to Baal, and my body's cravings would be his to sate.

Irina sidled up to us and addressed Erebus. "You were letting me win, weren't you?"

"I enjoyed your enthusiasm, and the view," Erebus said, a light tone to his voice.

Oh god, was he flirting with her? And why did I even care?

Irina laughed throatily. "Well, enthusiasm is something I have in abundance."

Now she was flirting back. This was too weird, but pointing it out would make me look like I gave a damn, which I didn't. We still had a good few hours of riding ahead of us, time to switch off. Closing my eyes, I allowed their conversation to wash over me, blocking out the chest rumbling seduction and sultry tones. If those two were going to get it on, then I didn't need to know. The lulling rocking of the mount, Erebus's warm body pressed against me, and the trusted circle of his arms, made it impossible to resist the lull of sleep.

***

"Kenna, we are here." Erebus's lips grazed my earlobe, waking me with a shiver.

Cracking open my eyes I squinted at the blood red sky.

"Dawn approaches," Irina said. "We must get inside before we are spotted."

Erebus lifted me from the mount, but didn't set me on my feet, instead he carried me cradled against his chest, into a tumbled-down shack and gently lowered me onto a wooden chair.

The cabin was threadbare but clean. "I thought we were stopping at a tavern."

"The tavern is a mile up ahead. But this is safer," Erebus said. "It's a traveller's lodge kept stocked by the tavern. Employees of the crown—messengers, emissaries and the like—use it. Irina is stabling the mounts, and then she will place a cross on the placard outside to let other travellers know this lodge is taken."

So the fact I was here would remain a secret, and our mission with it. "Good plan." My stomach rumbled. "What is there to eat?"

I made to stand but he gently pressed me back into my seat.

"Let me take stock."

"Where? There is no kitchen."

He laughed and pointed at the huge pot hanging over a wide hearth. "That is the kitchen. I will go check the larder."

He wasn't gone long, and when he returned his face was a stormy frown. "It seems like the tavern has been neglecting its duties."

"Or maybe no one's been this way in a while?" I shrugged. "With Kai in power for so long there's been no official crown. This could have been the villager's way of snubbing a cuckoo king."

Erebus sighed. "Yes. But it means we have no food."

Irina entered the cabin, her gaze going from Erebus's annoyed expression to my resigned one. "Do we have a problem?"

"No food," Erebus said.

Irina grinned. "Just as well I brought my bow. I'll go catch us something. There's a brook not too far back if you wouldn't mind fetching some water, and your majesty, do you know how to light a fire?"

A week ago I'd have said no, but since assimilating with my alters I had a host of skills at my disposal. "Sure, I can do that."

Irina left us to our tasks and ducked out to hunt.

Erebus picked up the bucket by the door. "You'll be all right with the fire?"

"Will you be all right fetching water?"

His lips twitched. "Testy, aren't we?"

I growled in exasperation. "Just go fetch the damn water."

He headed out, his laughter a low rumble that left me aching. Fuck this efreet shit. Focus Kenna. Time to build a fire in the hearth and ignore the one building inside me. We'd be at the Black Forest soon enough, and maybe I'd get to vent some aggression there. Great, now I was hoping to get attacked.

A few minutes later, fire started, I sat back on my heels in triumph. Yep, I could have done that in my sleep. I'd probably done this hundreds of times over the course of my many lives. Dwelling on it now was a mind-fuck. Time to explore.

The lodge was small and cosy, two bedchambers, a bed in each room, and a washroom with an ancient looking pump, that yep, did nothing. Erebus would have to make another trip to the river for water to wash in, cos perspiration and was not a cool scent on me.

The door opened, and as if summoned by my thoughts Erebus strode in, Irina at his back. They were both flushed, and the remnants of laughter lingered around their mouths.

That dark twisty feeling was back again. "How long does it take to get water?"

Erebus hung the pot over the fire, unfazed by my tone, but Irina faltered, blinking at me in confusion.

Shit I needed to rein it in. I pinched the bridge of my nose. "Sorry, I get snippy when I'm hungry."

Irina smiled warmly. "Well we can certainly do something about that." She held up three dead rabbits. "All skinned and good to go."

"I'll chop them up," Erebus took them off her. "Have you got herbs?" Irina pulled a bunch of leaves from her pocket. Erebus looked them over. "Yes, they should do it."

He could cook too?

Irina shrugged off her coat and joined me at the table. "We should go over the plan one more time. I think we need a new contingency plan."

"What? You don't like the if-we-get-caught-run-like-hell plan?"

She didn't crack a smile and her golden gaze remained speculative. "You use humour to mask your unease."

"Yeah, it's called being human."

"But you are not human. You are djinn and Twilighter. Humour will not save us."

"Honey, if we get caught, nothing will save us."

She tucked in her chin, her gaze on the dark grains etched into the table. "If we are caught, if the Twilighters discover us, then Erebus and I will distract them. We will give you every chance to escape and you must do so. Promise me."

"No."

"What?"

"I'm not leaving you guys and running."

She grabbed my hand and squeezed so hard I had to stifle a yelp.

"You will run, and you will survive, because if Baal returns and you are not safe in the palace, then anything the Twilighters do to me will pale in comparison to what he will do."

"You're afraid of him."

She shook her head. "No. Just of what he will become if he loses you, and what he will do to those responsible. I promised to keep you safe, but you are my queen and I am obligated to follow your orders, which is why we are here, and why Baal is unaware. But as a friend I beg you to grant me this one request."

The earnestness in her expression, the tension in her body sent a shiver through me. "Okay. I promise I'll save myself."

She exhaled, and released my hand. "Well, now that is decided I feel the stew could do with a touch of magic to speed it up."

She walked off to join Erebus at the hearth.

Baal was going to be so pissed when he found out about this. But I couldn't make all my decisions based on how he'd feel about them. Being a good queen meant putting the people first. Their needs must come above mine. And they needed a queen. Cold fingers of doubt slipped around my throat. If I died, then the realm would be back at square one—torn apart by lords fighting over the crown—and the hoard would rapidly gain strength. Had I been wrong to ignore Irina and Davin? This was what he'd been trying to impress on me. This would be Baal's argument. They'd both be right. But by then we'd be back. We'd be safe. The dark djinn would be free, and we could chalk it all up to experience. It was too late to be questioning my actions now, but maybe it was time to stop thinking like a Fearless officer. My stomach flipped at the thought of standing on the side-lines and letting others risk their lives. It wasn't in my nature to hang back. But then once this was done, once we'd squashed Orin's takeover plan, there would be peace. There would be no need for Fearless.

In the meantime, it was my job to stay alive.

***

Irina's breath was slow and even beside me, but sleep was being a bitch and refusing to take me. The sting in my veins and turmoil in my head didn't help. Back in Lindrealm, I'd have taken my bike and gone for a ride to clear my head. Maybe a walk in the fresh air? No. We were meant to be undercover, and getting spotted was not part of the plan. But lying here staring at the ceiling was a pretty shitty substitute. Slipping out of the bed Irina and I were sharing, I padded out into the main room. It was lit with an amber glow from the fire which still burned cheerily in the hearth. I'd sit and watch the flames until—

"Kenna?" Erebus stepped out of the shadows to my left.

I jumped, hand on heart. "What the fuck? Are you trying to give me a heart attack?"

He chuckled. "I was preparing some herbal tea." He held up a kettle. "Would you like some?"

"You drink herbal tea?"

"Only when I have trouble sleeping." His eyes glinted in the gloom as they raked over my sleep attire, which consisted of loose pants and a vest, not revealing at all, but under his heated gaze I may as well have been naked.

I parked my butt on the rug by the hearth and held out my hands to the flames, absorbing the delicious heat. "Stop looking at me like that."

Erebus hung the kettle over the flames and then joined me. "And what look would that be?"

His shoulder brushed mine, and I shuffled to the side, breaking contact.

"The one where you caress me with your gaze."

"Do you think I want to sense your every mood? The last few days you've been projecting your emotions and your desires like a beacon. I can feel your need like it was my own. It is impossible to ignore." His regard was a warm breath on my cheek. His tone dropped an octave, alluring and enticing. "I could satisfy your body's needs."

Damn him and his tempting offers. I blew out a breath and turned my head to lock gazes with him. "Like you did for Dante?"

His expression shuttered, and his silver eyes turned to flint. "I see you've been listening to rumours."

"So, you guys weren't intimate?"

He focused on the flames. "Dante was an efreet. She was passionate and wild and sexual. It was what made her a formidable warrior. But the blade wasn't enough."

"And you provided the extra?"

His jaw ticked. "Yes. And I would do the same for you. Dante was my princess, and you are my queen."

How could he say that? Did he honestly think he was worth so little? A cock to service his queen?

I laid my hand on his forearm, the skin taut and smooth under my fingers. "Yeah. You're right. I've been feeling different lately. The efreet thing is probably happening to me, but I can't just have sex with people to satisfy my needs. Fair play to the efreet that did things that way, but it's not for me. Maybe it's the humanity in me that makes me cringe at the thought. But even if I was to consider it, you mean too much to me to use you like that. You deserve better."

His breath caught. "Better?"

"Yeah. Someone who loves you."

"You loved me once." His words were a whisper.

Wow, had he really just gone there? "I honestly didn't expect you to say that."

He snorted. "Yes, neither had I."

I swallowed hard. I had loved him, still did. Just not in the way I loved Baal. Baal's face came to mind, his piercing green eyes and indigo hair, so soft and silken between my fingers. And then there was his wicked smile that made my heart race and my chest. But sharing my feelings with Erebus would be cruel. There was a time, not too long ago, when hurting him would have given me satisfaction. Not now. It was strange how living in this world for a while had changed my point of view, how it had given me a deeper understanding of the first djinn I'd fallen in love with.

Erebus sat up and reached for the kettle. "The tea is ready."

We drank it in silence, and then went our separate ways. Hopefully my silence was answer enough for his unspoken question.

<u>7</u>

The Black Forest stretched out before us, a vast expanse of darkness waiting to swallow us whole. Irina dismounted and led her leoequise to the edge of the forest. She patted its beastly head and whispered something into its ear.

I gripped Erebus's shoulders as he helped me dismount. "What is she doing?"

"Thanking it for the ride and asking it to wait for her."

"It understands?"

"Leoequise are highly intelligent creatures. They work with me because they chose to. They seem to have taken a shine to Irina." His lips curved in a soft smile.

There was so much about this world I needed to learn. Riding was one of them. I made a mental note to add that to the top of my to-do list, under save Lindrealm, protect the fifth dimension, and kill Orin.

Erebus strapped on his sword. The rest of the supplies would remain here with the mounts. Together we ventured forth into the forest. It was like stepping into a cave. The temperature drop was immediate, and the sun vanished. The environment was damp and musty and gloomy. Tall twisted tree trunks dotted our path, their branches entwined like a dying lover's desperate embrace. The leaves and flora were black or dark brown, and not a sound penetrated the thick, heavy silence.

"This is unsettling," Irina said.

"We have just over a mile to go and then we will reach the river," Erebus said.

A mile of this? Yeah, this would be fun. "Let's hope we don't come across any inhabitants of this place."

We trudged in silence, our breath fogging in the air as a residue of moisture settled over us like a chilly blanket. It was in my hair and suspended on the tips of my lashes. Damn, I missed the warm kiss of the sun on my face. How did anything live here?

A strange reedy noise cut through the silence, rising up to echo around us. Irina came to a halt, her arm up, hand in a fist. Erebus grabbed my wrist, arresting my progress. We stood, breath pluming in the air to join the thin mist rising off the ground, and waited.

Irina's shoulders relaxed, and she turned to face us, a reassuring smile lifting her lips. "I think—"

Something hit her from the side, swept her off her feet, and was gone, taking her with it.

What the fuck?

Erebus let out a yell and then we were both in motion, running full force through the forest, leaping over roots and crushing bracken beneath out leather boots.

Up ahead the shadowy form carrying Irina was still visible but moving incredibly fast. It was taking us off course, parallel to the river on the other side of this forest. Irina's limp body hung off the creature's shoulders like a sack of potatoes.

Thank god for my state-of-the-art prosthetic, the damn thing was almost bionic, but the rest of me wasn't, and I was flagging. Second wind required. Channelling the fire inside me, I forced it into my limbs, urging myself on. And then we were breaking from the cover of trees and into a clearing.

Erebus came to a skidding halt, and I put on my brakes. Irina was lying on the ground, in the centre of the glade, unmoving. The creature was gone.

"Erebus?" I took a step to stand beside him.

He scanned the area, his body tense and ready for action.

"It's a trap," Erebus said

"Yeah figures." The creature had lured us here.

Irina groaned and raised a hand to her head. "What…"

The same reedy sound we'd heard just before Irina was taken filled the air again, but this time I recognised it for what it was—laughter. They were laughing at us, whatever they were. The sound grew in volume, seeming to come from all around us.

We were surrounded.

Erebus moved quickly and hauled Irina to her feet. She shook her head to clear it and quickly assessed the situation. We fell into formation, back to back, circling, our eyes on the tree line around us. The prickle across my spine and the gooseflesh running up my arms told me we weren't alone. Something was watching. Several somethings.

And then they stepped into the clearing with us, cutting through the mist with their long snouts and yellow eyes. They stood on hind legs, mimicking our stance, but there was no way these things were human. And that laugh, damn if it didn't remind me of a hyena. They didn't attack though. It was almost as if they were waiting for something. And then it came floating into the clearing—a tiny light cutting a path through the mist. It skipped toward us and the creatures grew still and silent.

What the fuck was going on? The light hovered over Irina, then Erebus, and then came to settle on me. I batted it away, and the creatures growled and snapped as if enraged by my actions, but they still didn't attack.

Fuck this, I was queen and these were my lands. Even this shitty forest with these fucked up creatures belonged to me.

I lowered my sword and stepped forward, chin high. "Is this how you treat your queen?"

The light whizzed toward me again, and this time I didn't bat it away. It settled on my hand, the sensation warm and tingling, and then it floated back, growing larger and brighter until it was impossible to look at it. I turned my head away as a flash like lightning lit up the clearing, and then darkness descended once more.

"You are Ibris's spawn," a hoarse feminine voice said.

I blinked at the woman standing before me. She was practically naked except for a crude bit of fabric wrapped around her crotch, her hair was a long nest of tangles covering her breasts, and yet there was something almost regal about her bearing.

She'd called me Ibris's spawn. I locked gazes with her. "Yes. I am your queen."

Her lip curled and she growled low in her throat. "We do not have a queen. We do not have a king. We are the forsaken, the betrayed and the lost."

"What do you want?" Erebus asked.

She cocked her head. "We wanted fresh cock and cunt to swell our ranks. But instead we have found flesh, and with it, vengeance. We have the spawn of our enemy."

Vengeance? What the heck had Ibris done to them?

"You cannot hold your new queen responsible for the actions of her father," Erebus said.

"Yes. We can."

I looked to Erebus "Do you know what she's talking about?"

His jaw ticked and he shook his head slightly. "No."

The woman threw her body forward, and as her hands hit the ground they morphed into huge paws, the rest of her followed on a wave and then we were staring into the red eyes of the largest canine creature I'd ever seen.

Around her the other bipedal hyena-type creatures began to giggle. The sound grated at the inside of my skull, setting my teeth on edge. My muscles tensed, ready for action a split second before my brain recognised they were about to attack. Adrenaline surged through my veins, hot and potent.

Yes! This was what I needed.

The beasts attacked as one.

Erebus's roar of rage slammed against their laughter, turning it into snarls and hungry growls. Irina let out a whooping battle cry, and it was on. I slashed, spun, and jabbed. Fur split and sprayed blood. It painted my face crimson, heady and intoxicating. Yes! This was the ticket. This was what I craved. The thrill was an expanding bubble in my chest and my body moved on instinct, taking them down one by one. Yips and whines replaced the ferocious snarls.

"Stop. Stop!"

The female's plea cut through the red haze in my mind, and I faltered on an upward swing, pulling back short of eviscerating my opponent. Its claws whizzed toward my face. Arms grabbed me around the waist, pulling me to safety.

Erebus's voice was an angry growl. "Damn it, Kenna. Focus."

"Stop! Please!" The woman said.

The remaining creatures dropped to the ground and bounded away toward the tree line. The woman stood before us, her body a mass of welts and open wounds. It certainly wasn't my handy work. I glanced at Irina and then Erebus who both shrugged.

She stared at the carpet of dead beasts, and then placed her hands over her face and began to sob.

Oh fucking hell. I was so confused right now. "Seriously? You're gonna cry about it? You started this. You didn't have to attack us."

She raised her head, her red eyes blazing. "And your father didn't have to bind us to this place. But he did. He bound us. Look what we have become!"

Around her the hyena men began to whine softly, the sound rising up like a mournful cry.

"What are you talking about?" Irina asked.

The woman held up her hands, and several tiny lights emerged from the trees. They hovered a metre above the ground and hung in the air around her.

"We are close to home and yet so far," she said. "Trapped in this in-between place of darkness by your father. My people, the wisps, were refugees running from a mad Twilight king toward a new future under djinn rule. We travelled through this very forest to get to the djinn lands, only to be captured by Ibris's guards and presented to him. He was kind and listened to our plea for land of our own. For a place to call home. Orin had destroyed our forest home to build his city, and then when we'd protested he'd sent guards to eliminate us. But Ibris offered us a home. In exchange, I was to accept his attentions."

"Attentions?"

Erebus cleared his throat and it clicked. Attentions as in sex? My cheeks heated.

The woman watched me carefully. "He took pleasure from my body, so different from his djinn concubines. My twilight nature excited him. His attentions were enthusiastic, and at first I merely endured for the sake of my people, but I am ashamed to say eventually I began to crave his touch. He kept me locked away in a chamber for thirty days and nights. And I began to burn for him. I began to believe his pretty lies."

The mournful cry grew louder, and then ebbed.

"On the final day, Ibris's guards came in the dead of night. They woke me roughly, took me from the chamber and drove me to the edge of the forest. You can imagine my confusion. Why was I back here? I asked them. Where were my people? They threw me into the forest, and when I screamed and railed and tried to rush out, I could not leave. I was trapped."

Erebus inhaled sharply. I shot him a glance, but his brow was furrowed as if deep in thought.

"Some kind of spell." Irina said. "I sensed something as we entered, but now it makes sense. It's a barrier spell."

"Yes, and we have been trapped here ever since. At first we fed off the flora. It made many of us sicken and die. But the ones that survived realised that if our race was to continue we would need to evolve. Over the centuries, through selected matings, we have become what you see today. We are able to thrive on the flora and the flesh of djinn that pass through this dismal place."

My father had done this? I stared at the dead bodies of the beasts. If they hadn't just tried to kill me, maybe I'd feel more sympathetic toward them. Maybe I'd feel worse about killing her people, but there was no guilt in survival. Plus her tale was off. It didn't correspond to what I knew of my father or the king Ibris had been.

"You shouldn't have attacked." I stood my ground. "I'm sorry for you plight. I truly am, and if you'd asked me for help then I'd have been happy to assist you. But you chose to attack us. You chose vengeance."

She shook her head. "A century trapped in this dead place, a century scavenging and fucking our way to survival. What would you have done?" She swept a hand toward the beasts hunched on the ground around her. "These are my children." She tracked the lights surrounding her. "Our children."

The lights expanded, sweeping over the clearing until several more wisps joined her—men and women, but none as imposing as the woman with the loin cloth and tangled hair.

"Ibris did this to us," she asserted again.

"No." Erebus said. "I recall this tale. Or some of it at least. The wisps came to the palace, although I wasn't aware what you were back then. Ibris spoke of your leader, a most beautiful female. He was enraptured. He wished to make her his concubine. He hoped that once she'd lain with him she would become enamoured and agree to stay, but then one day she was gone."

"No. That is a lie." The woman said. "His guards took me and put me in the forest."

"Yes," one of the other wisps said. "Guards woke us in the middle of the night and brought us here also."

This was beginning to sound dodgier by the second, and a horrible suspicion began to form in my mind. "And when you were trapped here you were furious at Ibris, right?"

"Of course."

"And you attacked the djinn attempting to pass?"

"Yes, we did."

"What of the Twilighters?" I raised a brow. "Did you attack them?"

"No. Our anger is directed at Ibris and his djinn."

"And then a few years later Ibris was assassinated," Erebus said. He shook his head. "We wondered why our spies never returned when sent this route. Why our intelligence on Twilight and its mad king's movements was so thin. And now we know."

I lowered my everlight blade. "My mother is a Twilighter. She has nothing but good things to say about my father. They were in love. I don't believe this was his doing. Guards can be bought."

The woman blinked at me, her mouth parting slightly as if under a revelation. "You think this was Orin's work? That he paid those guards to do this to us?"

"You said you were fleeing from him," Irina said. "Is it such a leap to accept that he may have tracked you, found out about Ibris's plan to help you, and then turned it to his advantage?"

"Your presence in the forest benefited no one but the Twilight king," Erebus added. "Why would Ibris trap you in here? It would serve no purpose to him. In fact it just made his life more difficult."

The wisps began to murmur.

These people had been hurt by Orin. There was no doubt in my mind about that, but there was no time to fix this now. "I'm sorry about what happened to you. And if there's a way to lift the barrier and set you free I'll find it."

The woman let out a shuddering sigh. "All this time …"

Erebus lowered his sword. "Kenna we need to go. We've already lost too much daylight."

"I'm sorry. I truly am, but right now we have an important mission to complete, and we need to get going."

"You are headed to Twilight?"

"Yes."

"The forest is fraught with danger. Allow my children to guide you."

Her eyes strayed to the fallen, all bloody and torn.

A hollow sensation filled my chest. "I'm sorry."

"No." She sighed. "You did what you had to. They would have ripped you to shreds and we would have never known the truth of our confinement."

Erebus sheathed his sword and the remaining beasts bounded past us into the tree line beyond.

"Go, they will clear you a path to the river." She fell to her knees amidst the carnage we'd created, and the other wisps followed suit.

Erebus gripped my elbow. "Orin has much to answer for. Let's strike the first blow by liberating my people."

I nodded and tore my gaze away, swallowing the lump in my throat as Bella's humanity wrapped itself around my heart and pierced it with guilt. Orin would pay for what he'd forced me to do.

8

BRETT

Baal's office was a haven of privacy after the heat of all those gazes in the board room. Brett had held his own and kept his chin up, but their obvious horror had almost been too much. The impulse to punch them in their faces had been a difficult one to squash.

"They're mobilising salt trucks to the gates as we speak," Baal said.

Brett hovered in the doorway. "And what's the official story?"

"The truth. Finally. The people deserve to know what we're up against. They can't protect themselves if they don't know what's coming. An emergency broadcast goes out later today."

Brett glanced at the coat closet, their way back to Baal's residence and on to the fifth dimension to see Kenna. But as much as he wanted to see his friend again, he needed to be taking action. Lindrealm needed all the Fearless they could get, and despite the changes in his physical appearance, he was still Fearless.

"I'm staying here."

Baal smiled wickedly. "I thought you might say that so …" He strode over to his desk, bent down and retrieved a box. He placed it on the table. "I took the liberty of having this made for you." Baal slid it across the surface of the desk. "Go on, open it."

Brett flipped open the flaps and stared at the dark fabric inside. Was that what he thought it was?

He lifted the fabric out—huge items of clothing, large enough to fit his new frame. But not just any clothing, this was a Fearless uniform. If he'd still had tear ducts his eyes would have been misting up right now.

Baal cleared his throat. "I've promoted you to patrol leader, and I'd like you to be in charge of coordinating the defence efforts here in my absence."

"What about the chiefs? They're never gonna go for it. You saw the way they looked at me."

Baal shot him a wicked smile. "Taken care of. There isn't a human alive that can resist my persuasion."

He'd used his djinn mind control mojo on them? There may have been a time that this would have pissed Brett off. But not any longer. Lindrealm was about to be at war, and as far as he was concerned, Baal could mind control the fuck out of whoever it took to save their arses.

"Thank you." Brett laid the uniform back in its box. "It doesn't solve the problem about being out in public though."

Baal's eyes were filled with compassion. "I cannot speak for the whole population, but having lived among humans for some time, I have seen that they treat their heroes well, and when the broadcast goes out later you will be a hero. You sacrificed who you were to protect Lindrealm. The people will stand by you."

Baal grabbed a set of keys off his desk and chucked them at Brett. "Your new bike. It's been customised for your new form."

He really had thought of everything. "You were pretty certain I'd want to stay."

Baal shrugged. "You endured torture for these people. I assumed you may want to stick around to make sure it was worth it."

"You assumed correct."

"I'll let Kenna know what's happening."

"Tell her to focus on the fifth dimension. The hoard needs to be kept under control. I'll keep an eye on Lindrealm."

"I will pass that on, but you know Kenna, she's a woman with a mind of her own, and if Lindrealm is attacked, don't be surprised to find her by your side."

Brett chuckled. The sound was like gravel and broken glass. He clamped his mouth closed.

"If you need to get a message to me you can do so by sending me a text."

"A text?"

Baal smiled. "I had a friend and shamateck make me a little something." He handed Brett a small device, more a pager than a phone with a keypad to allow for texting. "I won't be able to respond, but I will receive your message, and I will find you."

"A tracker?"

He nodded. "I will speak to Caldwell about your cure."

Brett tucked the pager into his pocket. If anyone could find a way to reverse what had been done to him, it would be Caldwell—the man who'd created the serum. He'd take the antidote, but not until his world was safe from Orin. This form, although horrific, afforded certain benefits in battle. Benefits that he knew he'd have to draw on sooner than he'd like, because his gut told him that time was running out for Lindrealm.

9

The river was waist deep on me, but only came up to Irina and Erebus's thighs. We trudged through the icy cold and climbed up onto the grassy bank on the other side. Behind us the beast men cackled before retreating further into the forest.

Our escort had been the perfect deterrent, and we hadn't encountered any other creatures on our journey through the forest. Erebus pulled out the map tucked under his leather vest and studied it.

"Your friend has drawn a twisted tree as a marker," Erebus said. He scanned the bank to our left and to our right.

The river was long. The tree could be either way, and goodness knew how far up. Why had I thought we'd just be able to cross the river and find it straight away? The sun was making an arc through the sky, and it would be dark in a couple of hours. We needed to hurry.

Closing my eyes, I exhaled and tapped into the power inside me. Come on intuition, gut instinct, something … and there it was—a tingling in my right arm.

I opened my eyes. "This way."

"How do you know?" Irina asked.

"I don't. Not for sure. It's just a gut feeling."

We walked for long minutes. No tree. Okay, maybe I'd imagined the tingle. But then there it was in all its twisty glory—a strange distorted thing with a small copse of similar trees surrounding it. Erebus cleared a path, and we ducked through, twigs and dry leaves crunching underfoot.

"There." Irina pointed at the gaping maw set into the side of a mountain. "These must be the sewers. No longer in use, thank god."

"I will lead the way," Erebus said.

He dove in and I followed, with Irina taking the rear. The sewers may no longer have been in use, but the stench of shit still lingered.

"It reeks," Irina said.

"Breathe through your mouth," Erebus said.

Yeah, that was still gross. Damn it was getting dark in here. Irina muttered something, and the tunnel ahead lit up with an amber glow.

"It won't last long, but it should get us to where we need to be," she said.

It was sweet of her, because I knew she could see just fine in the dark, so could Erebus, but despite the power inside me, my body was still mortal, and my eyes had their limitations.

We turned left at an intersection and the sewer smell receded as the terrain changed to a dryer, less dank atmosphere. We were in the tunnels Brett had told me about, which meant …

"Up ahead," Erebus said. "Above us."

The dark djinn were being held in a chamber somewhere above us. Maybe we could do this without using the invisibility potion Caldwell had created. We were almost there, I could feel it.

Up ahead Erebus's footsteps came to a halt. "Here."

Irina and I hurried to catch up. Erebus stood with his head tilted, staring up through a grate in the ceiling. His chest rose and fell erratically.

"They are here," his voice was a whisper. He laced his fingers through the square spaces between the bars and tugged with all this might. "It is solid."

Was I the only one noticing how small the damn grate was? There was no way Erebus was getting up there. No way Irina would make it either.

"Here, try this." Irina passed him a vial. "It's a corrosive agent that activates when in contact with metal. Just use the applicator to dab it onto the bars."

Erebus set to work, and with a hiss the bars began to dissolve. One tug and the grating came away. Dust and stone fell to the ground and we jumped back. We had an opening. Erebus stared at it, the reality finally clicking into place.

Irina cursed.

It looked like this mortal body would come in useful after all. "Hoist me up."

Erebus shook his head. "We don't know what's up there."

"If there were guards they'd be on us by now with the level of noise we just made." I grinned. "I'll be fine."

Irina took out the other vial. "Take a drop of this, just in case."

I stuck out my tongue and she squeezed a drop onto it with the pipette. My body tingled.

"Did it work?"

Erebus's hand shot out to connect with my breast.

"Hey!"

"Sorry." He quickly pulled it back.

Irina snorted.

I looked down at myself, but there was nothing there. "This is disconcerting."

"Just give your brain a moment to adjust. It knows where all your limbs are. Just let instinct guide you."

Erebus was staring at me, but not at me. Irina was speaking to me, but not to me. And I was here, but not here. It was all too weird, and I was gonna be stuck like this for two hours. The sooner we got this over with the better.

"I'm ready,"

Erebus made a hammock with his hands. "Just get up there and find us a way in."

Using the boost, I hauled myself up through the grate. "Fuck!"

"What is it? What do you see?" Erebus called up.

"The vine; It's huge, and your people are tangled in it."

Something clattered onto the ground beside the grate. The iron dagger. Hopefully it was the vine that was keeping them unconscious and nothing else. Hopefully once I cut it away they'd wake up and be able to walk out on their own steam, because if they didn't we were fucked. But first I needed to find us an exit, and hopefully an entry point for Irina and Erebus. I scanned the room—covered in glowing vines and suspended unconscious dark djinn—and found a set of double doors hidden behind neon green plant-life. Cogs poked out from beneath the foliage, some kind of mechanism to open the door maybe? There was no escape that way. There had to be something else. Maybe another grate? Something larger? A circuit of the room had me thinking I was gonna come up empty, but then there it was—a circular hatch with a thick bar threaded through metal hoops to keep it closed. The bar slid out easily, and tossing it to the side I grabbed the hoops and hauled. Damn it was heavy. It fell open with a muted thud.

"What's happening?" Erebus called.

A ladder led down into the dark. "I think I found something. Hang on." I dropped down into the hatch and clambered into the dark. If anyone saw me … well they wouldn't because I was invisible. Ha. My feet hit the ground, and I was back in the tunnel but tucked into an alcove.

"Kenna? Kenna?" Irina's voice drifted down the tunnel to me. I followed her voice and found them huddled under the grate.

"I'm here."

Erebus spun round, almost knocking Irina of her feet.

I held up my hands, and then realised he couldn't see them. "Follow my voice. I found another way in."

My hum led them to the hatch, and then we were back up in the vine room.

Irina made a circuit, her eyes wide. "Look at the door. I doubt anyone has been in here for a very long time."

Erebus moved from djinn to djinn. "Give me the dagger."

I handed it to him and he headed toward the dark djinn closest to the small grate. The huge djinn hung suspended half a metre off the ground, his body parallel to the floor, arms dangling so his fingers reached for the ground. One slice and the vine began to wither and blacken. Erebus made more cuts and the body dropped a little, and then the vine disintegrated and the djinn fell to the ground with a thud. A low hum filled the air.

"Kenna?" Irina said.

"It's not me."

Erebus dropped to his knees beside his brethren. The djinn's chest rose and fell sharply and then he let out a soft groan.

"He's coming to," Irina said. "Give me the dagger and I'll start on the others."

Erebus handed it over, his gaze still on the djinn he'd just freed.

Irina set to work on the next djinn, but something was happening. The withering that had begun when Erebus cut into the vines holding the djinn was spreading.

"Irina, wait."

Irina paused. "What is it?"

"Look at the vine. I think it's dying. I think we must have poisoned it with the dagger."

Irina glanced at the blackness that was eating away at the glowing vines. "Erebus. We may have a problem."

And then the djinn began to fall.

10

"Shit!" I dodged the huge bodies while Erebus attempted to catch them. And then Irina sent out a wave of energy which hit the remaining falling bodies and slowed down their descent. They kissed the ground and began to wake up.

I sagged against the wall. "We need to get the heck out of here."

Erebus was busy helping the djinn to their feet. They chattered in a strange guttural tongue I didn't recognise. This wasn't the usual djinn language, because that one I understood fine.

Even Irina looked perplexed.

The dark djinn gathered together surrounding Erebus and blocking him from view. There were hundreds of them. My pulse sped up. Hundreds of powerful warriors to add to my army, to face off against Orin.

The djinn parted and Erebus strode through with a powerful silver-bearded djinn by his side.

Erebus swallowed. "Kenna?"

"I'm here."

The silver-bearded djinn balked.

"It's all right father. Kenna is under the effects of an invisibility potion. She is also Ibris's only surviving heir and our queen. Kenna, this is Baronus, leader of the dark djinn tribe and my father."

The man, Erebus's father, inclined his head. "Your majesty. We are honoured that you came to liberate us."

"I couldn't let Erebus have all the fun."

He blinked rapidly, as if surprised by my response, and then his silver eyes, so like his son's, lit up. "In that case, maybe we can have some fun during our escape."

I let out a bark of laughter. "I was thinking more of a stealthy getaway. But trust me when I say we will get vengeance for what has been done to you."

He inclined his head once more.

"We should go now, before our luck runs out," Irina said.

Erebus began herding everyone toward the hatch. Irina slipped down first to lead the way and then the djinn began to descend. Around us the vine continued to die, blackening and withering. There was only a small expanse of glowing plant remaining. My gut twisted in warning.

"Erebus, hurry it up."

He looked over his shoulder with a frown.

The final glowing vine died, and my heart skipped a beat in foreboding. and then the room was filled with an eerie high-pitched scream.

"What is that?" Erebus asked.

"The plant, I think the plant is setting off some kind of alarm." The low hum in my ears made sense now. "I think the alarm may have started going off as soon as we infected the vine."

"Hurry!" Erebus ushered the final djinn down the hatch.

The vines were dead, but they clung to the walls and ceiling where they'd become lodged like ivy. The entrance shuddered with an impact from outside as Twilight guards attempted to open it. The only thing holding it closed was the vine. But the vine was dead … how long before it gave way?

"Kenna! Get down the hatch." Erebus scanned the room widely.

I took a step toward it then stopped. Once the guards got into the room they'd know for sure the dark djinn had escaped. They'd follow us down the hatch and into the tunnels, and any chance of us all getting out would be severely diminished. We needed to keep them out of the room. Keep them focused on getting in while the dark djinn escaped. My gaze slid to the mechanism by the door. A quick examination showed that it could be jammed. I just needed a metal rod or something.

"Kenna, come on!"

The bar that had been holding the hatch closed! The door shuddered, and I ran toward the bar I'd chucked to the side of the room.

"Go! I'm right behind you."

"I'm not leaving without you."

I slotted the bar into the mechanism.

"What are you doing?" He asked, his voice laced with impatience.

"Stopping them from opening the door."

"Good plan, now move."

I released the bar and stepped away. The door shuddered and held. Yes! I was almost at the hatch when the bar clanged to the floor. Shit. One more shove and the crusty vines holding the entrance closed would surely give way.

"Kenna, we need to go now!"

"Go. I'll be right behind you. I need to reinsert the bar."

"Dammit, woman."

"Not woman, your majesty. I'm your queen and I'm giving you an order. Go. Now!" I picked up the bar and slotted it back through the mechanism to jam it. Shit, I was gonna have to hold the damn thing in place.

"Go, Erebus. That is a fucking order from your queen."

Erebus looked down the hatch and then across at the door, torn.

"I'm invisible and resourceful. I'm Fearless."

"Dammit Kenna. I'll be back for you."

He dropped down into the hatch and the door shook. The vines tore and slid to the ground. Shit, now I was the only thing holding this door closed. The bar slipped, but I pushed it back, holding tight as another shudder shook the doorway.

Irina and Erebus should have cleared the sewers by now. Just a few more minutes to make sure and then I'd—

The door exploded inward, throwing me backward. I hit the ground hard and guards swarmed the chamber. The hatch … I needed to get to the—

"No, this cannot be!" A figure strode in, dressed in fine robes, his long silver-blonde hair falling down his back in a silken sheet.

"The tunnels!" The liveried guards jumped down the hatch.

"Your majesty." One of the guards inclined his head. "My men will find them."

This was Orin? Twilight's king, who hoped to take over Lindrealm and the fifth dimension?

"Then what?" Orin asked. "You will find them and then what will you do?" His lip curled, and his eyes flashed. "Fools. Useless fools." He touched the signet ring on his finger. "Find them and bring them back to me." His tone was velvet soft, almost seductive, and the guards backed up, eyes wide with fear.

The temperature in the room dropped. I picked myself up and padded stealthily toward the open hatch, but it vanished behind a veil of smoke.

"Majesty, please …" The guard pleaded.

"Hush. There is nothing to fear. The Hunt rides."

Shit. Where were they? Not here. Then outside? In the tunnels? It didn't matter. Erebus would have made it to the forest by now.

I'll come back for you.

Shit.

I had to warn him. The fog was thinning and the hatch was visible again. I took a step toward it, and a shiver ran over my skin.

"What do we have here?"

I turned my head to find Orin's gaze on me. Right on me as if he could … Shit. He could see me.

I was so screwed.

Orin's gaze lingered on my face and his eyes narrowed. "Arrest her."

An icy wind blew the remnants of fog toward them, warding them off. Hands gripped me around the waist.

Baal.

"I've got you," his voice was tight with anger.

I'd take it, and the tongue lashing that was sure to accompany it, because we were out of here.

11

We landed on the outskirts of the Black Forest. "What the hell were you thinking?" Baal snapped.

I threw my arms around his neck and pressed a hard kiss to his angry mouth because this was a conversation reserved for later.

He exhaled shakily. "We will discuss this later."

"Fine. But right now we need to get to Erebus. Orin released The Hunt to go after the dark djinn. We need to warn the others."

Baal was instantly on alert. "They're in the forest, heading for the fifth dimension as we speak."

A howl drifted up out of the woods, and icy fingers clamped the back of my neck. "It's inside the woods. The Hunt is going after them. We have to do something."

Baal wrapped me in his arms and took to the night sky. The vortex of air that surrounded us made it impossible for me to see anything. Were we close? Had The Hunt found Erebus and Irina yet? And then we were descending. My feet touched ground, the cocoon of air died, and my ears were assaulted with howls. The sound was coming from up ahead, and then it was joined by a united battle cry. Baal gripped my hand and we ran.

The Hunt had found the dark djinn.

We stumbled into the clearing, the same one where the wisps had accosted us, except this time there was no sign of the wisps. Instead, dark djinn swung their swords to ward off dark shadowy figures that slipped and morphed and attacked. To my left a dark djinn exploded into ash and to my right another froze and then imploded.

The Hunt was a pack of wolves, then a pride of lions, and in the next moment it was a giant bear. The djinn slashed and stabbed, but their weapons were useless against a force that couldn't be maimed. Orin had asked The Hunt to retrieve the dark djinn, but they were killing them. It made no sense.

For now The Hunt's attention was on the dark djinn. Erebus and his brethren were the ones in danger. Baal and I weren't the target. Orin had ordered them after the dark djinn and they were here to collect. There had to be some other way to get rid of them aside from salting the earth. Could Irina's magic help? Shit, where was the battle mage?

"Baal? We have to find Irina."

We spotted her on the edge of the clearing, lying prone, head to one side. A large bruise the size of an egg bloomed on her forehead.

Baal gently lifted her into his arms. "Irina? Irina, can you hear me?"

She moaned and opened her eyes and stared up at him blankly, and they her gaze filled with comprehension. "The Hunt!"

Baal set her on her feet, keeping his arm around her to steady her. "Is there anything you can do?"

"No. I tried. This is something beyond my comprehension."

Another djinn vanished in a spray of ash. We were fucked. The Hunt wouldn't stop, not until they'd achieved their objective. My hand went to my everlight sword and Baal grabbed my elbow.

"No. Your life is too valuable."

"Sod that, I'm not going to stand here and watch them get slaughtered." I shrugged him off and dove into the fray, my sword cutting a swathe through the darkness. Around me the dark djinn fought back to back, side to side. Their blows were ineffectual, but there was no giving up. They'd fight until all their people were gone. I caught a flash of Erebus's silver hair, the whites of his teeth bared in exertion as he hauled a dark djinn out of harm's way and missed getting slashed by a hairbreadth.

My heart sank. This was futile; a fight we could not win. And then the air was filled with cackles. Could it be?

The upright hyena beasts erupted into the clearing through the trees, their fur glowing eerily in the darkness. Behind them floated the lights—so many tiny orbs. They attacked as one, hitting The Hunt head on. The hyenas slashed and snapped with their glowing fangs and claws and the lights zoomed into The Hunt, swarming like a multitude of fireflies.

The Hunt faltered and then turned its attention on this new threat, the dark djinn forgotten. Whines and growls took over the night as The Hunt attacked the wisps and their offspring. I fell back with Baal at my side.

A wisp zoomed toward us. "Go. Go now." It was the woman's voice, the wisps' leader.

"We can't leave you like this."

"You must. We will weaken it enough to force it back, but it will take the remainder of our power. This is the end for us. But it is one we choose. Consider it penance for all the djinn lives we took. Now go."

Erebus called out to the dark djinn in that strange language and they began to retreat. I made to follow, but then Baal had me in his arms again and we were airborne.

***

We landed on my balcony and I shoved him away stumbling into my room. "What did you do that for? We should have stayed with Erebus and the djinn. What if the wisps fail to stop The Hunt?"

"Then you will be safe here in the palace." He strode back onto the balcony. "You may have been able to order Erebus to do your bidding, but I am not your lackey." He turned away and vanished in a whirl of air—probably headed back to check on Erebus and co.

God, I hated my lack of justification for being pissed off. He was right. If I'd died today, the fifth dimension would have fallen into chaos once again. But still, did he have to be so harsh about it?

In hindsight, waiting for Baal to get back and formulating a solid plan may have been the wiser move, but he'd have talked me out of going. He would have made me accept that I was needed here as the figurehead of peace. The Fearless inside me craved the thrill of the hunt, and I'd let it take the lead on this case. Not to mention the damn efreet fire that burned in my veins.

If not for the wisps, we'd all be dead. They'd sacrificed themselves to save us, and it was suddenly clear why Orin had chased them out of their home. He must have known that they were able to fend off The Hunt. But then why trap them in the Black Forest, the main route from Twilight to the fifth dimension? If he'd ever intended to attack us, he'd have had to send The Hunt in that way. Maybe he'd been banking on the wisps hating djinn so much they wouldn't have cared, or hoping they'd just wither and die. But the wisps had proven to be more resilient than that, and now they were gone. Was this our fault? We'd climbed into the lion's den and yanked on his tail. We'd prompted Orin to release The Hunt and it had resulted in the wisps being wiped out. But leaving the dark djinn in Orin's hands hadn't been an option.

The night sky glared back at me accusingly. "Fuck you, sky!" Maybe Davin would provide a distraction until the others returned. After all, we did have a coronation to prepare for.

***

Davin was in my office hunched over a bunch of papers, working by the light of a crackling fire and a single lantern. Yeah, I had an office, more of a library really—who knew that Ibris had been such an avid reader?

Davin looked up from the papers he was reading and exhaled in relief. "Thank goodness Baal found you," he said.

"I was wondering how he'd figured out where I was."

Davin smiled. "You gave no express instructions not to pass on the information."

Yeah, I'd impressed the do-not-tell-Baal on Irina, but failed to do the same for Davin, which was kinda a good thing, because it had saved my skin.

"He got to me just in time. Thank you."

Davin inclined his head. "You're welcome."

I walked around the monolithic desk and looked down at the paperwork, all squiggles and lines. "Whatcha doin?"

He held up the scroll. "Checking the guest list." He picked up another scroll. "Organising seating."

My brows shot up. "Seating? For the coronation? Why can't people just sit where they want."

He choked back a laugh. "Do you wish to keep the hoard silent?"

"What's the hoard got to do with seating plans?"

He sat back in his seat, pen in hand. "Organising such an event is similar to organising a wedding. You must look at the history of relationships between the parties and place them accordingly. For example, I would not place Overlord Phenex beside Overlord Zaghan, their families have been feuding since before our world collided, something to do with a marriage alliance gone sour and an unfortunate death."

"Well, I wouldn't know. I've never had to organise a wedding before."

"I was responsible for managing Kai's social events."

And now he was managing mine. "Look Davin, you really don't have to do this. I can get someone else to takeover."

He looked up horrified. "What? After all the effort I've put in so far?"

I grinned at his exaggerated expression. "Fine. You can keep the wonderful job of seating plans and guest lists."

I threw myself into a wingback by the window and stared out at the twinkling stars. "You were right, you know, I don't think I should have gone with Erebus. Baal is furious with me."

Davin turned in his seat to face me. "Is that the only reason you now regret your decision?"

Regret my decision? "Oh gosh no, I don't regret going." I filled him in on what had happened. "If I'd stayed at the palace we may never have found out the truth about the wisps, and Erebus and Irina may have been killed. And even if they'd made it through the Black Forest, they would never have made it through the small grate and into the chamber, and if by some chance they'd found their way in, then Erebus would have had to stay behind to hold the door closed, and I doubt Baal would have gone back to save his arse."

Davin chuckled. "So, you going contributed to the success of the mission."

"Yes it did. But still. I was thinking like a Fearless officer, not a queen, when I made the decision to leave."

The firelight caressed Davin's handsome face and his lips parted in a warm smile. "I believe there is a reason for the existence of every creature, and a purpose to every event. You were meant to go on this mission. You were meant to survive. As queen you will come across many difficult decisions and choices, and a good leader not only listens to their head but also heeds the counsel of their heart."

"So in other words, I did good?"

He let out a bark of laughter. "Yes, you did good."

It was strange sitting across from him—the first djinn I'd ever met. I'd been sixteen at the time and I'd saved him, and now he was on my team. Maybe he was right. Maybe there was a purpose and reason for everything. Maybe Karma wasn't always a bitch.

I stood and pulled my chair over to the desk. "Well, come on then. If I'm going to do this queen thing, I need to know my public. Tell me about the Overlords."

Davin picked up the guest list.

***

There was still no sign of Baal two hours later. The journey back to the palace on foot or beast would take at least a night and a day, but for Baal, who travelled on the wind, it was a matter of minutes. But he still wasn't here, which meant he'd either decided to travel with them or had gone off to do other shit.

Gah! If this was his way of punishing me for keeping him out of the loop, then it was working. Where was Fargol when you needed him? I would have flown off to find Baal myself if my gargoyle friend was here. Prosthetic off, I swung my legs into bed and pulled the sheet up to my waist. Sod waiting up. I closed my eyes. Long minutes passed and eventually the knots in my body unwound and my breathing evened out and slowed.

A body pressed against my back, warm and familiar. A hand trailed down my arm then slipped round to cup my breast.

Baal.

My heart kicked up and my annoyance melted away under the immediate heat of my desire. I arched my back and pressed my ass into his crotch. I was so ready for him, wet and warm and tight in all the right places. He rolled my hard nipples between finger and thumb, tugging gently and sending sharp shock waves down to my core. I ground into him, urging him to take those clever hands south, and like the obliging lover he was, he did just that, skimming my abdomen and then pressing the palm of his hand to my crotch and dipping in with his fingers. Oh god, fuck yeah. He played me and I danced, moving against his hand, gasping and moaning as the pressure built until I was shuddering and panting and mewling with release.

So good, but I needed more.

"Baal," I turned to him and wrapped my arms around his neck, pulling his lips to mine for a kiss.

He pulled back, his cerulean eyes dark with desire and something else I'd come to recognise as concern. "You could have been killed."

His tone was soft and un-accusing, as if he was stating a fact. But I knew better. I'd heard him use the same tone just before verbally ripping an opponent to shreds. There was no point arguing just for the sake of it, plus the orgasm he'd just given me had left the world soft and hazy.

I caressed his cheek. "I know. I'm sorry."

He exhaled through his nose. "I wasn't expecting that. Maybe we should precede all potential arguments with an orgasm."

I smiled. "I'm sorry I went without telling you, and I kinda know it was a bad idea, but I had to go."

He brushed back my hair and sighed. "I understand why you felt that way. It's your nature to lead in all things including battle, but our biggest battle is with the hoard, one that can only be won by your soothing, reassuring presence on the throne as queen. The people need you, Kenna. You make them feel safe, and we need them to feel secure if we are to tame the hoard."

"But if the hoard was keeping Orin away, then either way, we're fucked."

"All we can do is focus on one issue at a time. Orin will come, there is no doubt about that, and when he does we will fight him. The land surrounding the realm is being salted as we speak. The Hunt will not set foot in the fifth dimension again. Erebus is travelling here on foot with his brethren, and I've taken Irina to Caldwell to aid him in creating an anti-serum. Once we have it, we can use it on Brett and any modified denizens that crawl into Lindrealm. We'll take away his advantage, and then we will attack."

"You have it all figured out, don't you?" I ran my thumb across his full bottom lip, my body tightening as his breath hitched. "There is something you need to get on right away though."

His brow furrowed. "What?"

I leaned in, ran my hand down the length of his hard cock, and whispered. "Me."

His chest vibrated in a chuckle, and then I was on my back and he was obliging.

12

BRETT

Everything in his house looked just the same as he'd left it, complete with a coffee mug sprouting mould. The trip to Twilight seemed a lifetime ago, and here he was, a monster in his own home. Baal had been right. The announcement had done the job. He was a hero to his people, but it didn't change the flash of fear in their eyes when they looked at him. Being feared sucked. It was lonely and isolating. Lauren was the only person he'd come across that looked him in the eye without flinching. Baal was excellent at masking his reaction, and Kenna, bless her, had done her best, but it was Lauren who made him feel almost human. In his presence he forgot what he'd become. But Lauren was gone, back to Twilight and the black mages, back to doing whatever the group did to gather intelligence and work against a tyrant king. And Brett had a job to do to.

He climbed the stairs, boards creaking under his bulk, and squeezed through the door into his bedroom. The bed looked like a child's toy. No way would that hold his weight. He yanked off the mattress and threw it on the floor, then lowered himself onto it. There was no need for a duvet. He no longer felt the cold. He no longer felt anything. But he was determined to sleep, to do something normal, even though he suspected that sleep was no longer a necessity. Tomorrow was a big day. It was his chance to rally the troops, to inject urgency by telling them his tale first-hand. The Fearless needed know what they were up against, what they were fighting for, and the Academy would be packed with every Fearless officer in the city.

He closed his eyes and drifted.

Low malevolent laughter pulled him back to consciousness. He opened his eyes to gloom and dankness.

"Shit."

It was the damn cave again. His gut contracted in fear.

The laughter echoed toward him, taunting. "You cannot escape me, human."

He'd been wrong. He was capable of feeling something—bone numbing terror. Time to get the heck out of here, but just like the last time, he was unable to move. No. He was not getting stuck down here. He had a job to do. Lindrealm needed him.

Shadow tendrils seeped out of the inky black maw ahead of him, curling and twisting their way toward him. He wasn't sure how, but he knew if they touched him then he was lost.

"Do not resist, do not delay the inevitable," the wicked voice said.

"Nope, delaying sounds good, thanks."

The creature chuckled. "I will so enjoy you."

"Who are you?"

"I am the father, the mother, the womb. I am chaos and order, and I am hungry."

Well that was certainly an introduction. "What do you want?"

"To feed."

Made sense. Was this supposed to be his fate? Had Orin somehow tied him to this creature, whatever it was? Maybe there'd come a time when he'd be too weak to fight it, but that time wasn't tonight. He had too much to live for.

"Sorry, my soul is not on the menu." Ice filled his veins, searing cold, and then he was in motion, stumbling away from the tendrils and avoiding the brush of death.

It was time to wake up.

The creature's bellow of rage filled his head, and when he opened his eyes the plain white ceiling stared back at him.

He sat up, heart pounding. He needed to tell Baal and Kenna about this. There was no doubt in his mind now that this thing, this monster, was real and somehow connected to Orin. It was something they hadn't factored into their defence plan. And that needed to be remedied ASAP.

Hauling himself onto his feet he thudded out of the room. There would be no more sleep tonight.

***

Message sent via pager, Brett made his way to the Academy. The bike Baal had provided was perfect for his new height and breadth, and for a little while he pretended he was himself again, flesh and blood and on a case. But one glance down at his fingers curled around the handlebars was enough to shatter that illusion. And soon he'd be the focus of almost one hundred Fearless Officers. He fixed his attention on the winding lane bordered by wild brush and foliage. Magick was potent here, seeping in from the other dimensions and settling into Lindrealm soil. The scent was heady and lifted his spirits. Funny, he'd never noticed that magick had an aroma of its own before, but he was no longer human and his senses were now otherworldly.

The Academy came into view as he reached the top of a rise. It sat in a lush expanse of greenery surrounded by the crazy magick-infused woodland. The bike hurtled down the road, bumping onto the dirt track that cut through the forest. Branches slapped at his shoulders and scraped at his face. He picked up speed, flying over roots and brush, and for a brief moment his heart was gripped by exhilaration, and then he was flying across the grass toward the imposing Academy where the future of Lindrealm waited.

The Fearless would fight. No doubt—it was their fate, their destiny. But to save Lindrealm they needed to be prepared to die. It was up to Brett to convince them of that.

<u>13</u>

A monster stared back at me from the mirror. Puffed sleeves, smothering lace, and ruffles in places ruffles didn't belong.

Behind me Baal choked back his laughter. "You look ... impressive."

"I look like an overdressed peacock."

The maid stepped back as Baal approached me and placed his hands on my shoulders. "It's just one day. People expect a spectacle at a coronation, and it has been a couple of centuries since their last one. A century since there was any real reason for celebration." He leaned in, his lips brushing my ear and sending a delicious shiver through me. "And afterwards I get to peel it all off, layer by layer."

Yep, that would do it. "Fine. I'll wear the dastardly dress."

His lips twitched. "I promise to make it worthwhile." He caught his bottom lip between his teeth. "If I didn't have to go pick up your mother I'd give you a preview."

My face grew warm and I couldn't help but smile. "Go fetch my mum. I'll see you at dinner. Heather can help me out of this."

"Lucky Heather." He met my gaze in the mirror, his pupils large with desire.

My pulse responded with a trot. He cupped my shoulders, brushed the base of my throat with his lips, and then released me. He exited the room, leaving me trussed up like a Christmas turkey.

The maid, Heather, stepped into the space Baal vacated and set to work on the millions of buttons running down the front of the outfit.

I pinched the bridge of my nose. "Oh lord. Did Ibris wear something like this when he was crowned?"

She stared blankly at me.

I exhaled sharply. "It's fine. Just get me out of it please."

In a few hours Mum would be here. She'd always intended to join me, just wanted to put her affairs in order first. But with Lindrealm under threat I'd convinced her to come immediately. Sod getting affairs in order.

Back in my usual slacks, teamed with a crimson leather corset-thingy, I was about to head out to find Davin when the air around me grew completely still. My hand went to my everlight sword.

"Kenna?"

The hairs on the back of my neck stood to attention. I knew that voice—familiar and beloved. My eyes pricked, and I spun to face Sabriel.

My guardian angel beamed and held out his arms, not that I needed an invitation. I was on him like a shot, hugging the crap out of him. He smelled of sunlight and summer days, and damn it was good to have him back.

I gave him a punishing squeeze. "What the fuck took you so long?"

He made a melodic sound, which I recognised as a chuckle, and stroked my hair soothingly. "Red tape. There was plenty to cut through, but I'm here now, and I'm not going anywhere." He gently pulled back to look down into my upturned face. "I see you've achieved much in my absence." His lips lifted in a half smile. "Power looks good on you."

I snorted. "Hardly. I think I prefer the Fearless existence over this. You should see the dress they want me to wear to the coronation."

His sapphire eyes twinkled. "I can imagine. But it is simply a dress, and it is simply one day."

"Yeah, Baal said the same thing." He'd also promised to peel the damn thing off me afterwards, but Sabriel didn't need to know that.

"Baal is here?"

"Yes." I winced as his fingers tightened on my shoulders

Sabriel eased his grip but the tension didn't leave his body.

"You have a problem with Baal?" A distant memory triggered, and I struggled to grasp it. Yes, he'd asked me to be wary of Baal. I smiled and pressed a hand to his chest. "It's fine. Baal has been awesome. In fact, if it wasn't for him I'd never have made it this far."

Why did he seem to be getting tenser with every word that fell out of my mouth? He took a step back and turned away, head bowed, hands on hips as if in contemplation.

"Sabriel, what's wrong?"

He shook his head. "Nothing. You and Baal have obviously become good friends?"

Was he fishing to find out what kind of relationship I had with Baal? Was it even his business? But then, Sabriel was my friend. "It's a little more that, well a lot more. Baal and I are together." I smiled. "I'm in love with him."

Sabriel's face blanched. He muttered something under his breath, something that sounded an awful lot like fucking red tape. But angels didn't curse, did they?

"Sabriel, what the heck is going on? You look like you've seen a ghost."

He ran a hand over his mouth. "I feel like it. Listening to you is dredging up memories I've strived to bury."

"Memories? What kind of memories, and what have they got to do with Baal and me?"

He exhaled through his nose and glanced heavenwards, as if hoping for some divine intervention or sign.

My scalp crawled with foreboding. "Dammit Sabriel, just spill it already."

"I cannot. It would constitute as interference."

My belly quivered in warning. Drop it, it said. But I had to know. "Damn interference, Sabriel. If this concerns me then you need to tell me. Now."

"Kenna, I … I can't …"

Sod this. I didn't have the time for persuasion and guessing games, and as much as I adored Sabriel, I had no room in my court for people who kept secrets from me, however noble their intentions.

I straightened my spine. "I chose to surround myself with people who I can trust, people with my best interests at heart, and people who won't keep secrets from me. If you're not one of these people, then you have no place here." It hurt to say it, but I bit out the words anyway and stood my ground.

"Kenna …" His expression was conflicted, and then he exhaled and took a shuddering breath. "You had a sister called Dante."

I rolled my eyes. Was that it? "Yes. I know."

He blinked, looking taken aback. "Did you know that she was betrothed to Baal?"

"Yep." My shoulder muscles unknotted. This wasn't so bad. He was probably worried that I'd find out Baal had loved my sister and be all upset about it. "Baal told me how much he'd loved Dante. But he loves me now."

Sabriel's lips twisted as if in pain, and then he took a step toward me. "Baal may have loved Dante, but she didn't love him. She loved Erebus, and when Baal found out he killed her."

Had he just said killed? Baal killed Dante? Blood rushed to my head and my pulse pounded in my ears.

"No. Baal loved her. Erebus and Dante … they were just a thing for a while before she fell for Baal."

"Is that what Baal told you?"

"No. I have no idea if Baal knew about Erebus and Dante, but Erebus confirmed he'd been intimate with her."

"Yes, Erebus was intimate with Dante, both before and after she was betrothed to Baal. Baal discovered the truth and killed Dante in a rage."

He was talking about the guy who'd risked his life to save me, who'd shown me kindness and lifted me up from the bowels of despair. He was chatting shit about the man I loved. I'd never seen Baal lose his temper or go into a rage. Baal was composed, cool, calm, and rational. Everything I desired.

Anger ignited in my chest. "Why are you doing this?"

He blinked at me, taken aback. "I speak the truth. Baal is responsible for Dante's death. He killed her after he discovered she was in love with Erebus."

I shook my head. "No. No he wouldn't do that. He's not a murderer, especially not for such a petty reason. We don't control who we love."

"But love can drive the sanest man crazy. It can make us act and think irrationally and make us do things that … shameful things that eat away at us for eternity."

"How the heck do you know anyway?"

Sabriel's lips tightened. "Because Dante was my friend. She died while I watched."

Dante's death wasn't Sabriel's fault, and yes it was unfair, but there was a pot of lava simmering inside me, desperate to eat away the words he was uttering. "Well some fucking friend you are! Watching her die and doing nothing?"

He flinched as if I'd slapped him. I fisted my hand to prevent myself acting on impulse and doing just that. How dare he spew such awful accusations? How dare he attempt to take away the one good thing in my life?

The look of horror and sorrow on his face should have made me feel bad, but he was cutting at my soul with his accusations. I couldn't—I wouldn't—lose Baal.

The dismay on Sabriel's face melted into something twisted, and his next words showed me it was self-loathing I was seeing. "You think I wanted to stand by, invisible and silent, and witness her death? I am chained by what I am—an angel unable to interfere. She was my friend, and I was forced to remain hidden and watch her die."

His pain penetrated the haze of rage surrounding me and my throat grew tight. "How? How did she die?"

"He pushed her. Baal pushed her off the edge of their world."

The edge of Baal's retreat. His haven. The place that he'd built for Dante … or had he? Had anything he'd told me been the truth? My heart screamed at me to deny this knowledge. I loved him, dammit.

I loved him.

"I'm sorry, Kenna, but there is more."

"Fusksake, what more could there be?"

His expression grew even darker. "After Dante's death, I was forbidden by the powers that be to speak of what I had witnessed, but I kept a vigil on Baal. The weeks leading up to Ibris's assassination, Baal made two trips to Twilight."

What was he trying to say? And then it clicked, and my heart squeezed painfully in my chest. "You think he conspired with Orin? You think he wanted Ibris dead?" I took a step back. "No. He wouldn't. They were friends."

The tremble in my knees and the racing of my heart screamed that this was too much. Sabriel had gone too far.

Sabriel snorted. "Friends? Maybe to begin with, but over the years that friendship soured under Ibris's neglect and ignorance of what was required to run the realm. Baal was the true force behind keeping the fifth dimension running smoothly. I even admired him for it. It was why Ibris offered Dante to him. He knew Baal was in love with his eldest daughter and recognised Baal's growing dissatisfaction at the lack of recognition he received for everything he did for the kingdom. Dante was meant to sweeten the pot. But Dante's heart rested elsewhere."

A flare of anger toward my long dead sibling had me gritting my teeth. "But she agreed to marry him anyway?"

"She knew what was at stake. Baal was a formidable ally, but his army was vast and he would have made a terrifying enemy."

"So she lied to him. Pretended she was into him."

"She was a dutiful daughter. She agreed to the match and even attempted to break her connection to Erebus, but love is not so easily quelled."

As strong as my desire to dismiss his words was, it was impossible to deny the truth in them. Baal had told me himself that he'd run the kingdom for Ibris, but the man Sabriel was describing was a far cry from the one that I'd fallen in love with, and there was still stuff that didn't make sense.

"If Baal was responsible for Ibris's death, then surely he would have made plans to take the throne. Why let Kai take the advantage?"

"You think the people would have thought kindly of Baal if he'd taken the throne immediately? No. He had to win them over, make them fight alongside him against a tyrannical ruler. Kai is not well liked. With Erebus's aid, Baal had hoped to claim back the city."

The night in the library at the fortress in Evernight came to mind. Baal had tried to convince Erebus to join him in claiming back the royal city.

"But Erebus had already taken an oath to protect Lindrealm."

"Yes," Sabriel nodded enthusiastically. "And so Baal's carefully-laid plans unravelled, until you came along."

No. Was he suggesting I was a pawn in Baal's bid for the throne? To accept that would be to accept our relationship was a lie. It was enough that my lover was a murderer, but to intimate that he'd also faked his feelings for me … the hope inside me withered.

"You love him," Sabriel said. You would marry him, and he would have what he always wanted. He would be king."

Why was I entertaining any of this? Oh yeah, because the words were falling from an angel's lips. Could he even lie? I slumped onto the bed, head in hands. Probably not. Bile crawled up my throat and I clasped my trembling hands together. Shit. Fucking hell. Baal … My Baal had killed my sister and helped orchestrate the death of my father. Where was the rage? Why was there only a hollow pit of nothingness, a growing darkness, and icy chill?

"You must beware, Kenna. Do not reveal you know the truth."

My head whipped up. "You have to be kidding me. You can't spill all this shit on me and then expect me not to clean it up. I'm not playing games. If Baal is this … murderer you say he is, this duplicitous, ambitious, power-hungry monster who will do whatever it takes to get the crown, then I need to know for sure. I need to look him in the eyes and ask him."

Sabriel made a sound of exasperation. "And what makes you think he'll tell you the truth?"

I stood. "He won't have to. I'll just know."

Sabriel grabbed my arm. "And he will know too. He'll know his ruse is up. If he doesn't end you, then he'll withdraw his aid in the fight to come. You need him Kenna. You need his army and his silver tongue."

I shrugged Sabriel off. "Then why tell me? Why not just wait till this was all over and then tell me?"

"To protect your heart. To give you the chance to shield it. Do what you must for the good of the realm, but protect your heart. Erebus broke it once, and I cannot bear for it to be damaged again."

"Too late."

A knock on the door was followed by Heather's tentative voice. "Your majesty, Lord Baal is requesting your presence in the library. Your mother has arrived."

"I'll be right there." My voice quivered. Everything I'd come to rely on, everything I'd known to be true and good, had just been ripped out from under me. Once again I'd been deceived in love, but this time the pain was deeper, soul-searing and breath-taking.

I loved him. My eyes burned and I squeezed them closed, taking a deep shuddering breath.

Queens didn't cry. Queens did what needed to be done.

It was time to face him.

How would I face him?

14

Laughter greeted me as I entered the library—Baal and Mum sharing a joke. Mum turned to welcomed me with a smile. Her jeans and shirt looked out of place and alien in this environment.

She took in my outfit. "Crimson suits you."

"Thanks." Don't look at him. Don't meet his eyes just yet.

"Kenna," Baal said, smooth and relaxed, as if he'd never pushed a woman off a cliff. "I was just telling your mother about the wonderful meal we've prepared in her honour this evening."

I fixed a smile on my face. "Yes, Baal has been hard at work, leaving his lordly duties to make himself available to me. He has become indispensable."

Baal's smile slipped.

Damn, I needed to dial down the cutting edge to my tone. Taking a breath, I glided across the room and gave Mum a hug, dropping a Baal a wink over her shoulder to diffuse the awkward moment. I was stressed with queenly duties and stuff, he'd get it. He got me.

His expression relaxed and he smiled. "I'll leave you both to catch up. Davin could do with some help finalising the travel arrangements for tomorrow's coronation."

Yes, the amphitheatre-type building on the other side of the realm. The streets would be packed with travellers; some guests, some merely hoping to catch a glimpse of the event of the century. We'd planned to ride together in the carriage pulled by Baal's water-horse friends, but the thought of being in close confines with him now made my stomach hurt.

"I was thinking maybe Mum and I could ride together, just the two of us." I grinned. "Some mother daughter time."

Baal made an 'O' with his mouth, momentarily thrown. After all, I'd kicked up a fuss about having him with me on the journey, and now I was pretty much dismissing him.

He recovered quickly. "Of course. I'll prep the Ceffyl Dwr."

He moved in to press a kiss to my forehead and it took everything I had not to flinch, and then he was striding from the room.

"Kenna?" Mum said.

"Yeah?"

"Is everything okay?"

The truth was on the tip of my tongue, but Sabriel was right. If Baal somehow found out I knew the truth about his past, then it could be dangerous for me and my loved ones. If I told Mum that Baal was responsible for my father's death, goodness knows what her reaction would be. It was best to keep this secret to myself.

"Everything's perfect. I'm just so happy you're here." I grabbed her hand. "Come on. Let's get you kitted out for tomorrow. You are, after all, the queen's mother. You need to look the part. The royal tailor is awesome."

He cheeks flushed. "Well, if you insist."

The rest of the afternoon was spent choosing fabric, gossiping, and reminiscing about Bella. She'd have loved playing dress up.

I was here because of Bella's sacrifice and nothing, not even my love for Baal, would stop me from being the best damn queen I could.

***

The throne room was packed with dark djinn. The edge of the vast room was lined with noble djinn and general populace. These kinds of events were called Open Court, and anyone could turn up and petition the monarch. In this case we had an army of dark djinn—some of the most powerful warriors in the realm, if I was to believe all that I'd been told. Even if I hadn't seen them in action myself, Erebus's skill would have been enough to convince me.

Speaking of Erebus, he stood at the front of the group beside his father, looking cool and composed after a fight for his life and a lengthy journey. In fact, they all looked unruffled and rested.

"Your majesty," Erebus's father inclined his head. "We have come to offer our allegiance. We will fight with you against the armies of Twilight."

"Thank you Baronus. Your allegiance means a great deal to the crown."

"Do not mistake me, your majesty. I do this not for the crown, but for the fierce woman who aided in our liberation and fought beside us when The Hunt attacked."

A murmur skimmed across the crowd.

Yeah, that wasn't something I'd planned on advertising, but it was out now. "I was glad to help. Erebus has been a mentor and a friend to me. His battles are mine."

"And now your battles are ours." He inclined his head. "We are honoured to fight by your side."

My eyes grew hot. Shit. Do not tear up. Queens did not blub. "Thank you Baronus"

Davin leaned in to whisper in my ear. "The dark djinn will need a home."

Of course. They were nomadic, but they'd been gone a long time, and if they were to fight for the crown then they needed to have a fixed place.

"Baronus, I would like to invite you and your people to stay here with us in the palace. There is plenty of room. Davin will make sure the guest houses are prepared and there are plenty of quarters in the west wing. Please take your pick."

Erebus's eyes flared in surprise. "We wouldn't presume to impose on the crown."

"I would be offended if you didn't."

"In that case," Baronus said, "we accept your most gracious offer."

I had the dark djinn army at my disposal—another feather in my cap. Another advantage in the war to come, but I'd lost Baal, and the emptiness within wouldn't be filled

***

I leaned back in my seat, fingers brushing the smooth wood of my overly large desk, and looked Erebus straight in the eyes. "Do you have a problem with me inviting your people to stay?"

"No. Of course not."

He was lying, I could feel it through our bond. I rested my clasped hands on my desk. The setting sun slipped below the horizon, and the dark djinn was painted orange and red.

"Erebus, what's the problem?"

"If they stay then so must I."

"And you have a problem with that, why?"

He locked gazes with me. "You know why."

My gut tightened.

"You forget that we share a bond. That your emotions, pleasure and pain, are also mine unless you mute the link." His jaw ticked. "You forget to mute the link."

Of shit. He was referring to Baal and my sexy time the other night. While he made the journey back to the palace, I'd been fucking the night away.

My neck was on fire. "I'm sorry."

He held up a hand. "It's not your fault. Neither of us asked for this. It was a necessity at the time. Distance acts as a muter, but being in such proximity to you makes the connection stronger. The tether is no longer a necessity, and if I am to remain here maybe we should consider severing it."

He thought I was going to be fucking Baal every night and forcing him to witness the highlights. If only he knew. "What about the hoard? The connection allows you to draw power from the flame inside me. It allows you to fight the hoard."

"And the hoard is silent. With you on the throne it is unlikely to surge. War is coming, and the people know this, but they also know we are prepared. There is very little potential for chaos and uncertainty."

He wanted to be free of me. I'd loved him once. But not anymore. No matter how much my heart ached for my loss now, there was no going back, it just wasn't my style. This was for the best.

"Okay, so how do we do this?"

His shoulders relaxed. "I will summon the priestess and ask her to prepare the ritual to severe the link."

A pang lanced through my chest. "Okay. When?"

"Tonight."

I dropped my gaze to the desktop. Yeah, this was the right thing to do, but with Baal taken from me, Erebus was one of the few real connections I had. But it would be wrong to hold on to him for selfish reasons. It was time to stand alone and make my own decisions.

"Kenna?"

I looked up. "Yes. Get it set up."

His brow furrowed and then he smiled softly "We do not need a cosmic link to be connected. I will be here for you if you should need me, link or no."

The knot in my chest eased a little. "Thanks."

***

"That was amazing." Mum flopped back onto my bed, hand on her stomach. "I forgot how wonderful fifth dimension food was."

She'd eaten djinn food? "You ate with Ibris?"

She sat up, and I noted the slight flush to her cheeks. "Yes. He smuggled me into the palace on several occasions. There was a room in a tower where we used to meet. Sometimes I would stay for days. We were very much in love."

"Why didn't he ask you to marry him?"

She ducked her head. "He did, on several occasions."

"So? What happened?"

"I said no."

I stared at her in confusion. "Why? You just said you loved him."

She picked at the embroidered throw on my bed. "I had my reasons, and it worked out for the best in the end. If I'd stayed I would have died, and you along with me."

Still, I needed to know why she'd turned him down. I opened my mouth to ask but she interrupted me with a nostalgic laugh.

"I remember there was one time we were in the tower together, and we heard voices. Ibris sprang into action and locked the door. We didn't usually bother because no one ever came up to the tower. It was a tucked-away space that we'd turned into our love nest. So anyway, on this occasion we were taken by surprise; it was obvious someone else had found out little nook. We pressed out ears to the door and heard Dante and Baal professing their love to each other."

What? "Baal and Dante? Are you sure it wasn't Erebus and Dante?"

She shook her head, her brow furrowing slightly. "No, it was definitely Baal and Dante. Ibris said so." She cocked her head. "What would make you think it was Erebus?"

Because Sabriel had said that Dante had loved Erebus. Gah, I so wanted to tell her, but Sabriel had been adamant I keep this to myself. "No reason, just … was this before or after Dante was betrothed to Baal?"

"Before. It was actually what prompted Ibris to offer his daughter's hand to Baal." She smiled. "Baal was always a trusted adviser and friend to Ibris. When I found out he was helping you, it put my mind at ease." Her expression darkened. "Losing Dante was a huge blow to Baal and Ibris. They both withdrew into themselves. But it gives me hope to see that it is possible to love again. Baal found that with you."

None of this made sense. "How did Dante die?"

She sighed. "It was a horrible accident. She fell from the cliffs outside her bridal home."

Sabriel had seen Baal push her …

"Baal was mad with grief. He locked himself away for months afterwards and would speak to no one, not even Ibris, his closest friend."

Irina had told me the same thing. "And then Ibris was killed."

She swallowed. "Yes. And I ran. Afraid for your life."

My head ached from it all. There was no reason for Sabriel to lie to me. He was my guardian angel. He'd risked punishment to take me to see Bella after she'd died. He had my best interests at heart, so then why was my gut firing warnings?

Mum placed a hand on my arm. "How have you been?"

Why was she staring at me so probingly? "Fine."

She smiled. "You took the flame, so I assume your efreet nature has surfaced."

"Yeah."

"And how do you feel?"

Was she referring to the high sex drive? "Mum …" I injected a warning into my tone. "I am not talking to you about that stuff."

She laughed. "Fine. But there is a way to sooth the ache if the most obvious solution isn't possible."

Now this I was interested in. "Go on."

She stepped out onto the balcony and returned with one of the liquorice blooms. "You steep the petals in warm water and then drink it."

I took the flower. "How do you know this?"

She caught her bottom lips between her teeth. "Ibris used it when I was away from him. He wanted to be faithful to me." He eyes glittered with moisture.

"Shit, Mum. I'm so sorry."

She shook her head, dislodging the tears. "It was a long time ago." She cupped my cheek. "He would have been so proud of you. Our love created something truly beautiful."

I reached up to touch my birthmark. "Except for this."

He lips tightened and her gaze hardened as if in determination, she took a shuddering breath, but a sharp rap on the door interrupted her.

I turned away. "Yes!"

Heather entered. "The priestess requires your presence, your majesty."

"What's going on?" Mum asked me.

"I'm getting untethered to Erebus."

Her brows flicked up. "Is that wise? There is still a war to come. Having that link could prove beneficial."

"It was his decision. Being connected to me, having access to my feelings and stuff, is hard for him."

Her mouth parted slightly and her face cleared in dawning comprehension. "He's in love with you."

I pulled her off the bed. "I don't know."

"Yes. You do. It's why you're doing this, even though you know the tactical thing to do is to maintain the tether. You're doing this to set him free and protect his heart."

Her words struck a chord within me. She was right. This was exactly what I was doing. I was protecting us both. What we could have had was now nothing but a missed opportunity. I'd given my heart to Baal, and even if he was the murderer Sabriel said he was, there was no going back. I would cut ties with Baal once this war was over. Punish him for what he'd done and move one. Pain lanced through my chest at the thought, and I bit back an involuntary moan.

I cupped my mother's face and pressed a kiss to her forehead. "Can you stop being so insightful for a bit?"

She sighed. "It's a curse."

I wrapped an arm around her shoulders. "I love you, Mum."

"Love you too baby."

***

Heather led me through the palace and down corridors I'd never seen, which wasn't surprising considering how huge this place was. It'd take me weeks to explore it all, maybe months. I bet there were a ton of hidden spots too, like the tower Mum had mentioned.

We took a narrow flight of winding stairs, and stepped onto a cosy platform decorated in lush purple fabrics edged in gold. An intricate, woven rug lay on the wooden floor, and a slender arched window looked out onto the palace grounds below. The maze could be seen from this vantage point, which told me we were at the back of the palace. A wooden door, varnished to perfection, faced us. Heather rapped on the door and then stepped back.

"Enter," the priestess called.

I stepped through into what was obviously her private quarters. Erebus and the priestess were seated on flat cushions across from each other. A table laid with tea was set between them.

"Your Majesty, thank you for coming so promptly," she said.

Erebus looked up from his tea.

"Please, call me Kenna."

She smiled. "An honour indeed. But it would be unwise for me to form that habit. I am an old woman, and should I forget and call you by your name in public, then it would be deemed highly ignorant. Better to make a custom of using the proper address."

Erebus looked up from his tea, his gaze slipped past me to settle on my mother.

I drew her into the room. "This is my mum."

Erebus stood to greet her, his body eating up space. "It is nice to meet you."

"Likewise. Kenna told me you trained her to fight with her prosthetic?"

"I simply helped her regain her confidence."

Mum smiled. "And I am grateful to you. I believe that people cross our path for a reason, to guide us, to love us, to tempt us, or simply to walk by our side until the path ends. I'm glad that my daughter found a friend in you."

Something shifted in Erebus's expression, and some of the darkness seemed to seep away.

The priestess clasped her hands together. "Shall we untether you?"

I nodded. "What do we have to do?"

She bent down and poured a cup of tea then handed it to me. "Drink."

Okay. I downed the slightly bitter concoction.

The priestess sighed. "All done."

What? "That's it?"

Erebus indicated his empty cup. I drank mine.

The priestess chuckled. "What were you expecting? A ritual? Chanting? Dancing naked beneath the moon? Although we could still do the latter if you wish."

I held up a hand. "No, that's fine. So this tea … what does it do exactly?"

"The tether that binds you is a cosmic connection existing on another plane. The herbs and magick will disrupt and gnaw away at the tether. It will take a few hours, but you will know when it snaps."

I tried to catch Erebus's eye, but his attention was fixed on the door. Probably eager to get back to whatever it was he'd been doing.

"Okay, thank you." I turned to the door.

"Kenna?" Erebus said.

I paused and glanced over my shoulder. "Yeah?"

"I'm still here if you need me." His smile was soft, transforming his harsh face into a new kind of mesmerising.

"Thank you. I will."

Mum led the way out of the priestess's chambers, and Heather led us back to my suite of rooms. In a few hours it would be over. The bond I'd shared with

Erebus for the past few months would be gone. The priestess said I'd know.

How would I know?

15

"You look beautiful," Mum said, fingering the ruffles at my sleeves.

"Mum, you need your eyes checked."

"No," Sabriel said. "She is correct. The colours and the cut flatter you."

I cocked my head and studied my reflection in the mirror, and yeah, now that I took an unguarded moment to assess it, the coronation outfit wasn't so bad.

"I guess it's all right." I shrugged.

"It will be perfect once the crown is placed on your head," Mum said.

A rap on the door and then Baal strode into my chambers, his expression serious. My heart lurched with joy, and then Sabriel's words came to mind, puncturing the joyous balloon expanding in my chest. How was I going to do it? How was I going to stop loving him? Surely knowing he'd killed my sister and possibly conspired to assassinate my father should have been enough. Then why wasn't it?

"Kenna," he took my hands in his. "I will have to leave immediately after the coronation."

I turned my face up to him. "Why?"

"A message from Brett. He says it's important and wants to see me."

Would Baal hurt Brett? No. What would that possibly achieve? Still … "I'm coming with you."

He tracked my features with his emerald gaze. "You will have hundreds of subjects wishing to speak with you, to mingle and know their queen. You will need to hold court, Kenna."

He was right, and asking him to wait wasn't an option. Brett wouldn't have asked him to come to Lindrealm if it wasn't important.

"Fine, but you need to get back ASAP and let me know what's happened."

He leaned in and pressed his lips to my ear, his voice a seductive whisper. "Keep the dress on until I get back. I always keep my promises."

He'd promised to peel it off layer by layer. Hot needles pricked my eyes. Where had that moment gone? Sabriel's eyes were narrow slits, his mouth tight. Yes. Baal was the enemy. I needed to remember that.

Fixing a smile on my face, I pulled back and injected a naughty twinkle in my eye. "Of course."

Although that wouldn't happen. I'd made Mum sleep with me last night, no reason why the girly time couldn't continue a little longer, and then I'd need to think of another excuse. He ran a finger down my cheek and my core tightened in response. Yeah. I needed to make up some of that damn petal water ASAP.

***

The palace was strangely silent as I made my way out into the private courtyard reserved for the monarch and her stables. Everyone who was anyone had already left for the coronation venue. It was an hour ride, and Davin had orchestrated it so that I'd arrive once everyone was seated. From the plans he'd shown me, this one day had taken up his every waking hour to organise. He'd taken this on without my asking, and damn I was grateful to him.

He'd gone on ahead to ensure everything went smoothly. It was the priestess's role to crown the monarch. Speaking of the priestess; I still hadn't felt the snap of the tether between Erebus and me yet. She'd said I'd know, but nothing strange had happened. If he'd been about I'd have asked him, but he was gone, along with the dark djinn. There was just a small group of us left—Baal, Sabriel, me, and Mum. Irina was still with her father working on the anti-serum, and Fargol hadn't returned from his gargoyle recruitment drive. Several guards waited on mounts, ready to set off as soon as we were safely on board. Baal would travel by air, using his elemental power to make his way to the coronation ahead of us, and Sabriel would do his angel thing and make his own way.

We waited in the courtyard, faces turned up to the clear blue sky waiting for my ride. The Ceffyl Dwr came into view a moment later, their hooves silently beating the air, clouds trailing behind them as they cut an arc down toward us. The white and gold carriage hovered behind them. How could I have forgotten how magnificently beautiful and wickedly terrifying they were? As they landed, trailing mist and snorting smoke, Baal stepped forward to greet them. They let him touch and whisper in their ears and then he opened the carriage door and held his hand out to me.

I slipped my palm into his but kept my gaze on the carriage. If I looked at him, into the face I loved, I'd be lost and the doubts would return. I couldn't do the circular argument any longer. Sabriel had told me the truth, and I needed to accept it. I needed to shield my heart. I made to step into the carriage, but Baal gently tugged me back, pulled me to him, and pressed his lips against my forehead.

"I love you," he said. "I'm so proud of you." He released me and stepped back.

A melodic caw drifted down to us, Baal looked up and smiled. I followed his gaze to see a long shadow circling down toward us, plumed and feathered and beautiful.

Agni grew closer and she began to sing. The melody was sweet and heart wrenching, bringing tears to my eyes and clogging my throat.

Mum gripped my elbow. "What is that?"

"It's Agni. She's a phoenix, the last of her kind. She used to be Dante's."

Agni circled once more, her song ebbing and then falling into silence. She made a final swoop and beat her wings, rising up and away.

An intimate warm smile played on Baal's lips, one that made me want to drop the ruse and rail at him, to slam my fists into his chest and demand he tell me the truth. I took a half step toward him, but Sabriel stepped forward, shattering the moment. He shook his head infinitesimally and then Mum was joining me, urging me into the carriage.

The interior was just as I remembered, plush and comfortable and luxurious.

Mum caressed the velvety fabric of the seats. "This is beautiful." She beamed at me. "Oh, Kenna. I am so proud of you."

The door slammed shut and we were in motion. Baal would be watching, waiting for me to wave goodbye, blow him a kiss something. But I ... I just couldn't. My heart was heavy but empty at the same time.

The carriage bobbed and then we were airborne.

"Kenna? Seriously sweetheart, what is wrong?"

I gripped the seat, fingers digging into velvet. "I'm just nervous."

"No. It's more than that."

I met her gaze steadily. "Honestly, I'm fine."

She leaned forward and placed a hand on my knee. "I'm your mother. I have been for several lifetimes and I know you, probably better than you know yourself. There is something bothering you, something to do with Baal. Tell me."

This was Mum. I'd never kept anything from her before. She'd shared in my every achievement and comforted me in my every failure. Her words had helped me find direction on more occasions than I could count. And I needed to share this. I needed to talk it out, so I told her. I told her everything.

"No." Mum shook her head. "I don't believe it. Not a word."

Hope ignited in my chest. "You don't?"

She pressed her lips together. "Ibris was an excellent judge of character. He was an intuitive man, and he trusted Baal with his life. Dante loved Baal with all her heart. Ibris told me that when he revealed who he'd chosen for her to marry she'd been ecstatic. I think that she may have had a sexual relationship with Erebus, but he wasn't her only conquest. Dante was an efreet. Ibris and I joked that Baal would have his work cut out keeping her satisfied."

"But Sabriel said—"

Mum held up her hand. "I don't care what he says. I don't believe it. He must be mistaken. Speak to Baal and trust your heart."

"I trusted my heart with Erebus and he deceived me."

Mum sighed. "I doubt he meant to do so. Love can sneak up on us when we least expect it. He may have loved Dante and lost her. And the next woman he gave his heart to was part of a plot to assassinate your father. You said he took an oath to protect Lindrealm, to atone for being blinded by his heart. He blamed himself for the deaths. I can understand why he may have hardened his heart. By the time he met you he'd probably forgotten how to feel. He put his oath first, and he hurt you. But that doesn't mean that your heart led you wrong. Erebus is a good djinn, but he isn't the djinn for you."

"But Baal is?"

"You know the answer to that. It's why you're so conflicted about what your angel told you. Trust your instincts Kenna. You have multiple lifetime's experience to guide you. Just speak to Baal."

She'd lifted a weight off my shoulders and lightened my heart. Subterfuge and lies and secrets weren't the way. I would look Baal in the eyes and ask him to tell me how Dante died. I'd know if he was lying. If he was the murderer Sabriel said he was then he'd pay, and if not, Sabriel would have some explaining to do.

A sharp twanging pain lit up my insides and then eased so suddenly it left me gasping.

"Kenna? Are you all right?"

I rubbed my diaphragm. "Yeah, I think ... I think the tether between Erebus and I just snapped."

The carriage dipped and the horses made a strange sound, a cross between a scream and a neigh. The coach swung from side to side. Mum slammed into the wall and I slid forward onto the floor.

"What the heck?"

"Kenna! Out the window, look."

I grabbed the window frame and peered out. The clear blue sky was dotted with shadows, huge malformed creatures with wings that beat rapidly like dragonflies. Long knobbly tails trailed out behind them. And were those pinchers?

Oh god, not again. The scorpion hybrid denizens that had attacked Baal and I after the Black Moon ceremony and almost killed us, and here were more of the same.

"What are they?" She stared at me in panic.

"Orin's creations. His henchmen." He must have found out about the coronation. Davin and I had believed we'd purged the palace of spies, but we'd obviously been overly optimistic. Dammit. If I'd let Baal travel with us … No. I was Fearless. I fought denizens for a living. Just not in the air.

Shit.

"What are we going to do?"

The horses decided for us, picking up speed and pulling away from the approaching threat. Their hooves churned mist into the hybrid denizens. Surely that would be enough to slow them down. A cloud formed behind us, blocking the flying scorpions from view.

We could do this. How far was the amphitheatre? The ground below was a blanket of tiny buildings and greenery. I had no idea where we were, no idea how much longer we'd be forced to evade.

Mum gripped my arm. "Kenna!" She squeezed, and pain shot up my limb.

The cluster of denizens hurtled toward us, not from beyond the cloud but directly from the side. How many had they sent, how were we going to evade them?

The horses screamed. The carriage shuddered and bucked.

My butt left the seat and pain exploded in my head as it bashed against the roof of the carriage.

"Kenna!"

Mum's arms were around me, cradling me as we slid from side to side. Pain bloomed in my shoulder and my leg. Mum's yelp was followed by a moan. We were lifted then dropped, and the world was filled with sunlight.

I raised my chin and stared up at the sky. My stomach dropped and ice invaded my veins. "Oh shit, oh fucking shit."

The roof was gone and the monsters closed in, pincers at the ready. A cool calm pervaded my senses and my hand closed around my everlight blade. Mum released me and scrambled back.

She knew what I was about to do.

I stood, legs planted wide for balance in a carriage that was swaying so hard it might as well have been a swing. My prosthetic locked, acting as an anchor. The denizens lunged and I sliced. My blade made contact with a pincer and glanced off with a scrape of embers. What the fuck? That blow should have dismembered it. It had certainly hurt them when Baal and I had been attacked. I jabbed again, and once again the blade glanced off the creature. No … Orin had done this. He'd upgraded the fuckers.

They were no longer vulnerable to everlight.

Mum's scream battered my eardrums. "Behind you."

I turned just as Mum slammed into me, trying to knock me out of the way, but she was too late. The huge pincher snagged us, plucking us from the dismembered carriage like a pair of juicy grapes. The appendage closed around us pressing us together, digging into my back. Couldn't breathe … I couldn't.

Mum's horrified face swam before my eyes and then darkness claimed my vision.

16

BRETT

Brett parked his ride and climbed the steps to the imposing Academy entrance. Nostalgia hit hard, stealing his breath as the memory of his first day flooded his mind. It seemed like a lifetime ago that he'd climbed these stone steps, a young man of barely seventeen years with stars in his eyes and hope in his heart. The hope remained, but the stars had winked out when they'd taken Danny from him and he'd lost Kenna. And now he was the star, the star of the show he was about to put on.

The doors opened and Fearless Holden, Brett's old tutor at the Academy, greeted him. The guy had barely aged. He looked as fit and toned as he had almost seven years ago. Holden didn't bat an eye at Brett's appearance, instead he smiled warmly.

"Thank you for coming Brett."

He led Brett into the foyer of the austere looking structure. Their boots snapped against the stone floor, echoing eerily in the silence. Students would usually be rushing about to and from classes, but today they were probably all gathered in the auditorium for Brett's big speech.

He knew the way to the auditorium but allowed Holden to lead the way, mainly because the corridor wasn't actually big enough to allow them to walk side by side, but also because he needed a moment to gather his thoughts and his wits. He was no stranger to morale boosting, had done it many times for his comrades, but this was different. This was about standing in front of his colleagues and the next generation of colleagues and having them examine his defects. Have them pity him for what Orin had done, and to turn that pity to determination to avoid the same fate.

The auditorium loomed ahead, and his heart rate picked up. He could do this. Just breathe and get through it.

Holden pushed open the doors and Brett stepped into the dimly lit room. Was that a kindness to him? To allow him to hide in the shadows while he spoke like a lurking beast? No, that wouldn't do. They needed to see. They needed to see it all.

Brett stopped in the doorway. "Turn up the lights."

Holden glanced over his shoulder, a question in his eyes.

Brett nodded. "Just do it. Please."

Holden reached for the switch by the door and the room lit up. A murmur rippled through those gathered. Brett took a deep breath and strode in.

Silence.

Pin drop silence.

And then someone began to sob.

Brett stepped onto the podium and looked down on his fellow Fearless. He could imagine what they saw. A beast of man, his bald translucent head gleaming in the lights, each harsh plane of his diamond cut face like a killing razor, and his eyes— eerie and empty save for the pinprick of a pupil. Yeah, they saw a monster who used to be one of them. Brett's chest rose and fell as he sought the best words to begin with. But then maybe words weren't necessary. He reached up and unbuttoned the shirt of the Fearless uniform Baal had given him. The custom-made attire that hid the truth of the mutation, under the fabric lay what remained of the man he'd once been. He slowly shrugged it off.

Gasps filled the air, and more sobs joined the first as they took in the taut flesh of his abdomen, unmarred until the diamond ate away at it, sliding beneath and leaving red swollen welts in its wake. The transformation had been halted, but his flesh was dying, failing against the assault of the mineral, hungry to claim him.

Brett locked gazes with a sobbing Fearless in the front row. "Stop." His voice was a slap.

The Fearless pressed a hand over his mouth, shaking his head. He was a newbie, probably only just graduated.

"You think I want your pity?" Brett swept his gaze over the crowd. "You think crying or gasping will change what's been done?"

Silence greeted him.

"This is what awaits each and every one of you. This is what Orin wants from us—our flesh and our bodies to form an army to take the fifth dimensions. We're nothing to him but cannon fodder for his assault on the djinn. He'll come soon, and he'll have mutated hybrid denizens and The Hunt to do his dirty work, and if we don't stand up and fight, if we aren't willing to die if need be, everything we hold dear, everyone we love, will be at his mercy. I know there are those of you who have clawed your way back after injury, eager to join the fight. There are other seasoned Fearless who would lay down their lives for the cause. But most of you are new graduates, cadets thrown into battle before your time, and my next words are to you. Yes, the threat is large, larger than we've ever faced, and the urge to turn and run the other way will be fire in your veins, but look at me. Look hard, because if you give in to that fire, this is what you're running toward."

He allowed his gaze to linger this time, making eye contact here and there. and then he locked gazes with a familiar pair of deep blue eyes. Eyes he'd looked into on several occasions as he reached climax, eyes usually filled with desire or longing, but this time they were filled with horror and disgust.

Karl lowered his lashes, breaking the contact, and for the first time since he'd been altered, Brett wished the diamond had reached his heart.

He was done here.

Slipping his shirt back on, Brett stepped off the podium and headed out of the auditorium. They'd get their orders soon. They'd been passed to Holden and all the bases—a city-wide alert to mobilise at the drop of a hat. The image of his altered form would stay with them now. It would haunt them, and when the time came they would do whatever needed to be done to prevent this fate befalling their loved ones.

Yeah, he was done.

17

"Kenna, baby girl, wake up."

Cool hands caressed my forehead. The coronation, the carriage, the attack! I sat up, eyes wide, breath exploding from my lips.

"It's okay," Mum soothed.

The room around me was constructed entirely of stone. Weak light shone in through the metal bars on the wooden door. "A cell. We're in a cell?"

Panic gripped my throat, nails digging into my flesh. Brett had been locked up like this. Experimented on. Is that what they intended to do to us?

"All right, so maybe it's not okay." Mum ducked her head. "But I've been thinking. He could have ordered them to kill you. This would be over, but he didn't. He ordered them to bring you back here so maybe … maybe I can reason with him. Get through to him."

I stared at her grime-smeared face incredulously. "You want to reason with Orin? The Twilighter who poisoned Brett and turned him into …" There were no words for what had been done to my friend. "Orin just orchestrated an attack on us. He's had us kidnapped. I'm the queen of the fifth dimension, an obstacle. If he doesn't want me dead, then he has something worse than death in store for me."

My hand went to my blade, but grasped air. Great. They'd taken Frieda, or had I dropped her? This was the moment when panic would be appropriate, but if I let that bitch in she'd never leave. Instead, I pulled myself off the ground and walked to the door to peer out into a stone corridor lit by a wall sconce. My coronation dress dragged across the floor behind me, cumbersome where it had torn during the attack. No guards, no signs of life.

I gripped the chilly bars. "We need to find a way out of here."

Mum joined me at the door, and pressed her hands to the wall. "We're deep down, sweetie. I can feel the earth above us—so many layers of earth. This isn't the palace. This is somewhere else, somewhere under Twilight."

Her words sent a chill up my spine. "It doesn't mean we can't escape. Plus, Baal and Davin will be searching for us. The carriage will arrive, all torn and stuff and Baal will figure out what's happened."

Mum's eyes grew dark. "The carriage won't arrive. I came to as they were bringing us down. I heard the guards talking. They mentioned executing the horses. They were laughing about a deception, something do with Kai."

My hand flew to my mouth. "They want everyone to believe that Kai had something to do with this?"

Mum nodded. "I believe so. But it makes no sense, because all that will do is cause discord and risk the hoard reactivating."

Shit. She was right. The hoard had kept the djinn realm safe from invasion for years, why would Orin want to reactivate it now? We were missing a crucial element of his plan. The only way to know for sure was speak with Orin, ask the right questions, and gauge his answers. A thought occurred to me, something Mum had said.

"Mum, what makes you think that you could get through to Orin?"

He gaze flickered from side to side. "I wanted to tell you last night, but—"

Boot falls echoed down the corridor, and Mum grabbed my hand in panic and tugged me away from the door, into the shadows in the far corner of the cell.

A face appeared beyond the bars—male with shorn dark hair. His skin was pale, almost translucent and black veins were visible like an intricate spider's web beneath it. His eyes were black, and slightly bulbous.

What the heck was he? Another one of Orin's experiments?

"Don't try anything," he said. His voice was like sandpaper scarping against my senses. "There's nowhere to run, and I have permission to hurt you if you try."

The click and clatter of keys followed as the door was unlocked. He didn't enter, just stood in the doorway and ushered me forward. He was alone. Could I take him?

"Don't," Mum's voice trembled. "Don't give him an excuse."

"Oh, please do," the man said. "We do love to inflict pain."

We?

Mum squeezed my fingers tight. "Please, Kenna."

Her fear was infectious. "I promise."

"Come." He jerked his head.

I stepped out into the corridor and Mum made to follow, but the guard slammed the door in her face.

"Wait!" Mum cried. "Take me too."

"You will not see him," the man said. "We permit him this one, as a reward for his service."

What the bloody hell was going on? Mum gripped the bars. "Kenna, there's something you need to know. Something—"

The guard slammed the handle of his truncheon through the bars, catching her in the forehead. She made an oomph noise, and then there was a thud as she hit the ground.

For a moment I was frozen in place, and then rage surged through my veins, taking over. My fist connected with the side of the guard's head. He stumbled back, steadied himself, and then raised his head to lock gazes with me. His lips slowly curled in a sadistic smile.

"We are so pleased."

Oh shit. He moved so fast I barely had time to react, and then his fist smashed my face, my eyes squeezed shut on impact. Something crunched and the world shattered into splinters of pain. I opened my lids to a red haze. The world was swaying and my face was a dull throb. Darkness hovered at the corner of my vision. No way was I going down. I shook off the impeding unconsciousness and spun, kicking him in the head. But my aim was off, something to do with being punched in the face. He laughed and lunged. His fingers gripped my hair, and he twisted. My scalp screamed in pain, reducing me to a wild cat, scratching and clawing at him to get him off.

He released me abruptly, the sneer slipping from his face.

I slid to the ground, my head throbbing and my face aflame.

"Get up," he said. "Follow."

He stepped over me like I was a piece of shit and began to stride off.

Using the wall as support I pulled myself up. Thank goodness for the state-of-the-art prosthetic, it was the only think holding me upright. My vision was blurred, and darkness threatened to eat away at what was left. My eyes grew hot as tears threatened. No. No. No. I was stronger than this. I could do this. Mum had wanted to tell me something, something that would help with Orin. With a clear head, I may just be able to figure it out. I hobbled past the cell, keeping my neck rigid. I wouldn't look into the cell. Mum was either unconscious or dead. If she was unconscious then I'd get answers when I got back. If she was dead … I'd rather not know.

And so I followed the guard and prepared my mind for an interrogation.

18

BRETT

Brett walked through the forest in his dream. The moon peeked from between the leaves, dappling the ground in silver. Up ahead the crackle and pop of a cheery fire lured him forth. Five figures sat around it, their voices a low murmur on the air.

Well, this was different, but he'd take anything as long as it wasn't the dank creepy underground cavern with the bone chilling voice that wanted to eat him. Yeah, this was new, and with the usual sense of malevolence absent, curiosity gripped him. He edged closer to the fire.

The murmurs stopped.

"You cannot steal up on us friend," a smooth low voice said. "We are the eyes and ears, the very breath of this place. We have been waiting for a traveller such as you. And now that you are here, it is time for us to tell our story. Come closer. Warm yourself by the fire."

There was no threat here. None that he could pick up on anyway, and his feet were taking the guy up on his invitation. Stepping into the glow of the flames he scanned the five faces, which in turn took him in. They were bland, almost too bland. No feature stood out, none that he would remember or comment on, and he found when he looked away the memory of the face blurred in his mind. Their clothes were plain dark fabric, wrapped around their bodies to stave off the chill that Brett didn't feel.

"Sit friend," another voice, this one gruff and older sounding, said.

Brett parked his butt on a boulder. "Who are you?"

"Weary travellers such as yourself, taking a rest."

No, they were more than that. "What is this place?"

The man opposite him looked about, as if assessing his surroundings. "It looks to me like a simple forest."

His comrade snorted in amusement.

They were toying with him, and his temper flared. He was curious, yes, but he wasn't in the mood to be made fun off. There was real shit to deal with in the waking word. "You know what? Sod this."

Brett made to stand, but a hand grabbed his wrist. It held him in place, unforgiving, like a band of steal. He looked down and caught a glimpse of bone, white and stark, poking out from beneath the dark brown sleeve of the male beside him, but in the next instant it was just a hand—a normal weather-tanned hand. Brett shrugged him off.

"Don't you wish to hear our tale?" The man on the other side of the flames said. His face glowed orange and yellow in the firelight adding the eerie edge that had, so far, been missing from this dream.

Brett's scalp prickled, which was strange because he was diamond-made now, but this was a dream so wasn't anything possible? The urge to get up and run was a tension in his thighs. But he held his ground, because his gut was warning him to hold fire—to stop and listen.

The man across the flames began to speak, and the already silent forest fell into a deeper hush, almost preternatural in nature.

"We came to this land when the first green shoot pushed itself free of the earth. We cultivated it, nurtured it, and it was our home. Our people were simple folk with simple needs and wants. We were a peaceful tribe with a harmonic existence. And then fire fell from the sky bringing it to us." He fell silent for a long moment.

Brett sat forward. "What? What did it bring?"

It was another voice that took up the story. "An ancient force we were ill equipped to face."

The fire cracked and popped.

"As the smoke died and the ash settled on the ground, we gathered our weapons of spear and bow and went into the blackened forest. There we found an abyss filled with darkness, and the darkness seeped out into our world, infecting and tainting flora and fauna, bringing with it fear and despair."

"As the land died, so did our hope," said a new voice. "We turned on one another. We became the darkness, and the darkness grew. It fed off our pain and discord. It drew strength from it. It was decided that the best of us would gather what provisions we could and go in search of aid. My brothers and I took on the mantle. We travelled for days, and yet no matter how far we went there was evidence of the darkness. It was a plague, a blight on our lands buried deep beneath our soil. We were beginning to lose hope until the world about us changed. The air stung our cheeks with a fresh briny scent and the ground grew green and lush. A mile or so more and we came upon sand dunes, and way ahead the great expanse of the mighty ocean. There were people here, living untainted and free. They took us in, fed us, and listened to our tale. It was through them we found salvation." He broke off and turned to the man to his left.

His companion inclined his head and took up the tale. "These people were no ordinary folk. They were sons and daughters of the sea. Related by blood to the ocean folk, their blood had a power we discovered could be used to save our lands."

Their blood? "What do you mean?"

The man speaking bowed his head and the one beside him took up the tale. "We discovered it was the essence of the ocean in their blood that kept the darkness at bay, and so we did the only thing we could. We slaughtered them all and collected their blood to purge the darkness from our lands. They were simple folk, peaceful folk. The kind of people we too had once been. With his last breath their leader placed a curse on us—to reap what we sowed. At the time we did not understand the implications of this curse. We returned to our people and spilled the blood we'd collected into the abyss. As the darkness retreated, as our people rejoiced, the curse of the ocean bloomed. The darkness wrapped its fingers around us, claiming the five of us as its final victims. We fell into the abyss, confidant in the knowledge we had saved our loved ones."

"But we were wrong." The first man continued the story. "From that day forth, on the night of the Hunter's Moon, we were forced to ride, to reap the souls of our brethren and feed the darkness below. It lives on, and now it awakens. We are slaves to the puppet and the master. We are never to be free, for the blood that could weaken the visitor is gone. The ocean people grieved themselves into oblivion, their tears seeping into and salting the earth. It is the only place we cannot walk. The rest of the world is doomed, because soon we ride. We ride and we reap."

"Our vigil must end now, but you must carry our knowledge from this place. Remember." Their voices rose as one. "Only the harmony of races can slay Legion."

The flames flared up, spitting embers. Brett's heart was pounding. The salt, the reaping, the creature under the ground, and Orin, it was all connected. He just needed to—

"The tale has been told. And our vigil is at an end."

The flames began to ebb and die. The forest around him began to wither and blacken and the men—fucking hell, the men were nothing more than stark white bone. Around him the trees began to crumble and the ground began to morph. The fire blew away in a whirl of ash, leaving nothing but cold dark earth and stone ... there was stone closing in around him.

No. Not again. Not the chamber. Not now, he had so much to tell Kenna. He had the key, he had the answers. He broke into a run, but something snagged the back of his shirt and the awful voice filled his head.

"I've got you now little pig."

19

We were going down. Further into the earth. Mum was right. I could sense the layers packed above and around us now. Thank goodness I wasn't claustrophobic. My face throbbed and it was difficult to breathe through my nose—pretty sure it was broken.

The guard stopped outside a door, pushed it open, and ushered me through. It was a lab of some kind. Various bubbling concoctions in a variety of glass containers were dotted around the room. Was this where Caldwell had worked on the serum for Orin? Speaking of Orin …

A tall broad-shouldered man stood with his back to us, his long silver-blonde hair trailing down his back. He turned to face us, his expression impassive, pupils large.

"Thank you Bernard, we are pleased. Leave now," he said.

The guard retreated, closing the door behind him. As soon as he was gone the man gritted his teeth and blinked rapidly. His eyes widened when they fell on me. He strode over and grabbed my chin. I tried to jerk out of his grasp, but the fucker was strong.

"Stay still," he said. "Do you wish your nose to remain at that angle?"

He grabbed it and I screamed. Something clicked, and then a cool soothing sensation infused my face.

"There. All better." He smiled down at me. His gaze lingered for a moment longer, focusing on my birthmark and then he stepped back.

My face no longer hurt. In fact ... I reached up to gingerly touch my nose—my perfectly intact, unbroken nose.

"We do not have much time. I'm Orin, King of Twilight, and I apologise for the manner in which you were brought here." Something akin to real sorrow crossed his face. "It cannot have you free to sow harmony. It must have chaos."

"It?"

His gaze flicked from side to side as if in panic. "There is so much, so much you need to know, but there is no time. I do not wish to hurt you." He took a step toward me. "The moments are few and far between now. I am gone for longer. I am tired, too tired, but you ... you can ..." His left eye twitched. "Remember that I would never hurt you." He turned his back on me, whispering furiously.

I couldn't catch the words. "Orin?"

This time when he turned to me he was like a different person. There was no warmth, no spark in his eyes. His face was a mask of nothingness, and when he spoke his voice was deeper, with a scratchy edge that coaxed gooseflesh to life all over my skin.

"Sit," he pointed to a strange, dentist-like chair behind me.

"Orin?"

His lips parted in a smile that made my stomach hurt. "Sit, Kenna Carter. Sit so that I may come to know you."

He advanced and I backed up, terror a real squirming entity inside my gut. This wasn't Orin, this was something else. The back of my knees connected with something. I stumbled and fell back into the chair.

Orin leaned in, his face inches from mine. "We enjoy guests. We enjoy learning them."

The thing, whatever it was, looked out at me from behind Orin's eyes. I sensed its presence, cold and alien and hungry.

He held up a syringe filled with black viscous fluid. "We enjoy being inside."

No fucking way. I pushed at his chest and kicked out, but he was immovable, a stone barrier, and there was no escape. His hand closed around my throat, pinning me to the seat, and then needle bit into my arm.

The black stuff. He was filling me with that black stuff.

He stepped back, his lips curling in a satisfied smile. "We will learn you, and you will join us."

My veins flared black beneath my skin with whatever poison he'd injected me with. Was it the same stuff that had fucked up the guard? Oh god.

"What is that? What did you put in me?"

"The connection. The essence of us."

"Is this the shit you used on my friend? On the emissary Lindrealm sent?"

"No. Your friend received a tiny taste mingled with a dose of servitude, this, what we offer you, is a gift. You will join us."

Fuck that. "You're delusional if you think I'll never join you."

He cocked his head then closed his eyes, inhaling through his nostrils. "You won't have a choice."

The conviction in his tone stamped at the hope in my heart. "Why? Why do you even want me?"

"Because you are important to him, and therefore you are important to us."

What the fuck was he on about? His face rippled and blurred, and I caught the flash of a familiar mark slicing down from his temple to cheek—a mark very much like my birthmark. I blinked and it vanished.

He glanced at the door and it opened. The guard strode back in.

"Take her back to her cell. We have her now, it matters not where she turns."

The guard hauled me to my feet. I wanted to fight, to push him away, but my limbs were heavy and hot. The world turned upside down as I was slung over the guard's shoulder and then we were on the move—back to the cell, back to Mum. Mum would have the answer. She'd help me fight this. I could feel the black goo inching up my spine, digging in its claws as it went, gaining a foothold. If it reached my brain I was gone. I knew it as sure as I knew that the sky was just a reflection of the damn oceans.

The guard threw me onto the stone floor. The urge to sit up, roll over, do something, was smothered by the paralysis in my limbs. The door clanged shut and the key scraped in the lock.

"Kenna!" Mum pulled me into her lap.

Alive then. Good.

"Oh, god, baby girl."

At least I could feel her hands on me; not numb then. It was comforting. Her face appeared in my line of sight, a bump the size of an egg decorated her forehead.

She smoothed back my hair. "Did you see him? Did you see Orin?"

My lips were immovable. The black gloop in my body was turning me into a sack of potatoes.

"They injected you with something." Mum picked up my arm to examine the network of black veins. "It's doing this to you. Okay, sweetheart, listen to me. Listen carefully. You can fight this. It's your body, and you have immense power inside you. He may be able to overpower your twilight power, but not the power of the flame."

How did she know this?

"Baby girl, trust me. Please. I'll explain everything, but first you need to burn this shit out of your system."

She'd said shit. She never swore.

"Use the flame. Use the power your father bequeathed you. He knew about you. He knew we were to have a child. After Dante passed, he wanted you to rule. He hoped for an alliance between the fifth dimension and Twilight. What better way than to marry Twilight's princess and sire the Twilight king's granddaughter?"

Wait what?

She stroked my face. "Orin is my father. Ibris didn't know, not until we got pregnant with you. I was afraid he'd spurn me. I was afraid my father would find a way to keep us apart. You're a Twilight Princess, Kenna."

The mark I'd seen on his face—the one so like mine. It made sense now. So many questions rushed through my mind. Why hadn't she told me this before? Was it Orin she'd been hiding me from? Had she known all along that her father was responsible for my father's death?

"I can see the questions in your eyes, and you will have your answers, but first you must purge your body of the taint. Use the flame, Kenna, find it and use it."

A tremor wracked my body and needles pierced my flesh. A scream lodged in my throat, impotent and choking. I gagged. Mum raised me up, pulling my back against her front and holding me tight.

"I'm with you baby. You can do this."

The flame. I needed to … Argh it was inside me, everywhere, sliding up the nape of my neck, making a beeline for my brain, as if it knew it was running short on time. It knew … Of course it knew. It must sense its destroyer lying in wait. But then the cell was rushing away, and I was slammed into a stone cavern.

What the heck?

I could move, and I was on my feet in an instant, alert and ready for whatever. My skin was pale and unmarred. This was the black stuff in my blood. It was tricking me, lying to me. Something scuttled to my left, and my hand went to my everlight sword, but of course it wasn't there. The drip drip of water drew my attention to the pitch black maw ahead of me. It beckoned and tugged at me.

Come here, come closer, join me, join us.

Shit! I slammed on the brakes, and laughter—cruel and sinister—drifted out of the aperture.

"Come now. Don't be shy." The voice was fingers on chalkboard setting my teeth on edge.

"Who are you?"

"I am many. And you will be many." The voice broke and splintered into a multitude of voices. "We are Legion."

Knowledge slammed into me, squeezing my lungs and stealing my breath—knowledge of the magnitude of this thing—the hunger and the potential to devour. It was an eater, an annihilator, and it wanted me. It wanted everyone. It wanted the world.

The darkness shifted and terror clamped a hand over my racing heart. No. I couldn't let it touch me. If it touched me then there was no going back. The flame. I needed my flame.

The fist around my heart eased and the flame hidden deep inside flickered and flared. Yes. Burn. I needed to burn.

The black entity inside me reached for my brain with its claws just as the flame exploded into a glorious inferno inside me, burning a path through my veins and annihilating the foreign body inside. Were those screams in my head? No. That was me. I was screaming. Fire filled my vision and seared my brain, and then the heat retreated, curling back into its box.

"Kenna." Mum's cool hands were on my brow.

"Mum."

My body was my own again—slick with perspiration but able to move at my will. I'd done it.

Mum pulled me into a hug, sobbing into my hair. "I thought I'd lost you. After everything I've done to protect you, I thought I'd lost you."

I pulled back, chest heaving, and pushed tendrils of sweat soaked hair off my face. "Tell me. Tell me everything."

20

BRETT

The alien evil thing had him by the cuff of his shirt, tugging him back toward the dark maw of the cave, its home, where Brett was certain it would strip the diamond from his bones to get to the juicy human centre. It would feast on his heart and entrails and devour the very essence of him.

He'd survived being turned into Orin's slave. He would survive this dream. Just a fucking dream, and there was no need for shirts in dreams.

The fabric melted away, and so did the thing's grip. Brett hurtled forward.

Wake up, wake up, wake up!

The thing was at his back, clawing, its talons scraping off diamond.

Please. No. Please.

"Wake up!"

Brett bolted upright, slamming his head against something that made an oomph sound. His heart threatened to burst through the layers of crystal encasing it, and his pulse raced in his veins as if completing the final stretch of a marathon.

"Are you all right?" Lauren approached the bed cautiously. "Brett?"

He was awake, back in his house on the mattress on the floor of his bedroom. "I'm awake."

"Yes, thank goodness. You were thrashing and whimpering."

The dream. The Hunt and the ancient evil. "I need to speak to Baal and Kenna, and I need to do it now!"

Lauren's lips turned down. "That's why I'm here. Brett, something's happened to Kenna." Lauren's words cut into his brain like shards of glass and sinister laughter echoed in his mind.

Brett locked gazes with Lauren. "We need to get to the palace, now."

Lauren held out a hand and helped to haul Brett up. "Baal feels you should remain here. The consensus is that Kai has her, a last-ditch attempt to stop the coronation and claim the throne. Baal and Davin are interrogating Kai as we speak."

"What makes them think it was Kai?"

"Kenna and her mother were travelling by air in a carriage pulled by water horses. When she failed to arrive at the amphitheatre, Baal and a party of guards took to the road to investigate. They found the carriage smashed to pieces from the fall. Scraps of fabric were caught on the shards of wood. It was Kai's crest."

"I thought Kai was wily and sly?"

"He is."

"Then I find it hard to believe Kai would send guards in uniform to kidnap Kenna. He would have hired an untraceable crew, or asked his guards to wear civilian clothing, And how did he pull the carriage of the sky?"

Lauren looked uncomfortable. "Baal is incensed. I do not believe he is thinking logically. There is considerable damage to the carriage. We believe it was shot down somehow."

"And the horses?"

"Gone."

None of this felt right. Coupled with the dream he'd just had and the knowledge he'd gleaned, the argument for Kai being the mastermind behind the kidnapping was circumstantial at best.

"Kai is the only one that will gain anything by taking Kenna."

"And he would know he'd be the prime suspect, regardless of whether they found any evidence pointing to him, so why risk it? It makes no sense." Brett shook his head. "No, there is something else that would gain from Kenna's disappearance."

"Something?"

Brett met Laurens gaze. "Yes. We've been pointing our fingers at the puppet while the master grows in strength. There is something under Twilight. Something that feeds off chaos and dissention, and

Kenna's kidnapping is going to give it exactly what it needs."

Lauren pressed his lips together. "This is about your dreams, isn't it?"

"It's everything to do with them."

"In that case, we best get you to the fifth dimension, and fast."

Brett was already out the door.

<u>21</u>

Mum leaned back against the cell wall, her gaze on the door. Her usually youthful face was suddenly lined with age in the low light shining through the bars. She looked weary and tired and old.

"Mum? You need to tell me what you know."

She licked her lips and nodded. "Yes. It's time. My mother, Aurora, used to say there was a time that father was a warm loving man, a time when he used to laugh with his whole face. He'd been handsome, even with the birthmark that ran from his temple to his cheek, a heredity marker handed down from generation to generation in his tribe. Mother said it was the mark that had drawn her. She said, in a sea of bland perfection he stood out like an interesting jewel. She told me they were happy. That he'd called her is heart. But I can't recall that time. The father I knew was often cold and distant, locking himself away in his chambers for days on end. The father I knew had no mark on his face, as if his association with the dark thing had wiped him of his uniqueness. And then there was the violence. He would fly into fits of rage at the drop of a hat. Mother took the brunt of it of course. On those nights when I helped by nursing her bruises and cuts, she would smile softly through her pain and tell me not to judge him too harshly. She'd say that he was not himself." Mum snorted. "But the self he showed us was the only version I'd ever known. He killed my brother, you know. Killed your uncle in a rage. My poor little Yule, he was barely five years old and Orin killed him. That was the day I stopped calling him father. I started to run away, stealing into the fifth dimension and losing myself in its wonders. It was how I met your father. He was at the Cinder market and we …" She blinked and sat up straighter. "No. That's not the important part." She wiped at her forehead, which was beaded in perspiration.

"Mum? Are you all right?"

"I'm fine sweetheart, listen. My mother told me that Orin was altered by The Hunt. That ever since he harnessed it he'd been different, as if a darkness had seeped into his soul. At first it had been little things, like the nightmares, and then the aggressive outbursts had begun. She told me that at first he'd begged her to run, to take me and leave. Go far away. But she'd stayed because she loved him, and by the time things got bad there was no escape. He wouldn't allow it."

"So what happened? Where is she?"

"He killed her."

"Oh god."

"The night before she died, she woke me in a frenzy, she said …" Mum's brow crinkled. "She said there was something inside him, that he wasn't alone in his head. I asked her if it was The Hunt. Maybe if we released The Hunt he would be free. She told me The Hunt had never been his and that it belonged to another, and Orin was merely borrowing it. That it was all a lie. Orin had been lied to and was truly lost. We made plans to escape, serious plans hushed and huddled in the middle of the night. She told me Orin was waging a battle and losing, that whatever had a grip on him would inevitably have all of him. I begged her to stay with me that night, but she said if she stayed it would arouse the thing's suspicions. She went back to her chambers." Mum sighed. "I never saw her again. In the morning Orin told me she was dead. Just like that, no emotion, nothing. And then he carried on eating his breakfast."

"Oh my god."

"I didn't want to believe him, of course. I searched the palace for weeks, thinking he'd hidden her away somewhere."

"Didn't you have a funeral?"

"Twilighters don't have funerals. When we die we turn to light, to luma, and disperse into the atmosphere."

Oh, I hadn't known that. "Your mother was right. When that shit was in my veins I went somewhere. A cavern with a deep dark yawning maw, and it spoke to me. It said it was called Legion. I think it's controlling Orin somehow." Yeah, he was technically my grandfather, but calling him that felt wrong. "I think it must control The Hunt too." I cast my mind back to the story Brett had told me, the one Orin's concubine had recounted, about how Orin had mastered The Hunt and saved his people. "What if Orin was tricked into letting this thing inside him? What if by taking control of The Hunt he unwittingly linked himself to it?"

Mother grasped my hands. "That's what I thought. But I couldn't figure out what it wanted. Because aside from driving my father insane, it seemed to serve no higher purpose. And then Ibris was assassinated, and I knew. This thing, whatever it was, had a bigger plan and it was using Orin to orchestrate it. If he wanted Ibris and his spawn dead, then what would he do to me once he found out I was carrying Ibris's child? So I ran."

"Why didn't you tell me all this before?"

"I was going to wait until after the coronation. Learning about Bella, accepting who you were and claiming the throne, it was more than enough for you to deal with at the time. I wanted to allow you to settle before I told you about your connection to Twilight. But I was wrong. Maybe if I'd mentioned this evil inside Orin sooner, we could have avoided being captured."

Ifs and maybes weren't going to help us now. "We need to get out of here. The djinn and the humans need to know what we're truly up against. You're right, this changes everything. If we can take out that thing, this Legion, then we can yank out the problem from its roots."

"It's here." Mums said, her eyes roving around the cell.

She looked pale, too pale, and there was perspiration on her top lip now. "Mum? There's something wrong. What is it?"

"I can feel it, Kenna. It's here, with us." She scrambled onto all fours, her hands pressed to the hard packed earth. "It's beneath us." She pressed her ear to the ground and closed her eyes. "Can you hear it?" She began to hum, low and even in the back of her throat.

An icy finger trailed up my spine. "Mum?"

She ignored me, continuing the eerie humming.

I grabbed her shoulders and yanked her up. "Mum!"

She flinched and the humming cut off. "Kenna. I'm …I'm so sorry." She reached up and cupped my face. Her hand felt different, softer, furry.

I jerked back and stared at it in horror. Her fingers were almost fused together, and fine dark hair covered her palm.

"What's happening to you?"

She blinked down at her hand. "I thought I had more time."

"Time? Mum?" An awful thought gripped my mind. "Did the guard come back when I was gone?"

She pressed her lips together and nodded. Her eyes welled and she blinked, dislodging tears.

"He injected you, didn't he?"

"Yes," her voice was whisper. "He said it was a super serum. No need for a second dose. That I'd be ascending soon. A soldier in Legion."

Oh god, oh god. "We need to get you out of here. We need to get to Caldwell's lab. They could have a cure by now, or be close." The door was hard and unyielding beneath my fists. The bars taunted me with their solidity.

"Kenna, baby, please."

There was no escape. None unless they allowed it. I was trapped and Mum was changing. They'd come for her, and when she was gone they'd come for me again.

"Kenna, listen to me. Orin, my father, is still inside there somewhere. Why else would he have captured us instead of just killing us outright? I've been thinking. It's why Orin went from asking mother to leave, to not letting her go, because the thing knew that as long as it had something that Orin loved, it would have its claws in Orin. And now it has us too."

That didn't make sense. "There were years when Orin had no one. Your mother was dead and you were gone … unless …"

Mum sat up, her eyes wide. "Oh, god, you think mother is still alive?"

It made sense. He'd called Aurora his heart, and if the thing had taken her then it would explain how it had managed to keep its claws in Orin for so long.

"Kenna, if this is true, you must find her. You must …Argh!" she doubled over, clutching her abdomen.

"Dammit, Mum." I pulled her into my arms, noting the fur on her arms and the strange hunch to her shoulders.

She raised her head, and I gasped at the strange yellow irises staring back at me.

"Please." She grabbed the cuff of my bodice.

What? No.

"Please, kill me."

I dropped her and shuffled back, legs tangling in the awkward dress. "No. We can fix this. Caldwell will have a cure."

She tucked in her chin. "There is no cure. Not for me. Brett didn't fully turn, so there is genetic material for the cure to work with, but for me … it will be too late. If you let the change run its course, I'll be lost." She raised her head and locked gazes with me. "Kenna, please don't let me be lost." She convulsed and dug her nails … not nails, talons, into the earth.

A low mewling sound filled the air. Me. I was making that sound, because she was right. There would be no saving her. Her body was changing right before my eyes. Her scream cut through my brain, rising in pitch until it was something all-together inhuman.

Oh god. If I didn't act now it would be too late.

"Kenna, please," her voice sounded muffled and thick.

She turned her head, her mouth filled with elongated teeth, her brows thick caterpillars.

Gulping back the tears and taking a shuddering breath, I lunged and grabbed her in a chokehold. I adjusted my grip, pressing down on the artery at the side of her neck,

He body grew still, and she looked up at me one final time. "Be strong, baby girl. Be strong. I love you."

She closed her eyes and drifted into unconsciousness.

Eyes burning, stomach in knots, I held on, pressing down on that damned artery for seconds that seemed to stretch forever.

I held on, even when I knew she was gone. Even then I knew she was dead

.

21

BRETT

Baal pinched the bridge of his nose with bloody hands. It was Kai's blood no doubt. Brett waited patiently for the djinn to absorb everything he'd just recounted. Erebus stood by the window, and Davin and Lauren had taken seats by the desk. Brett chose to stand by the door. The room seemed too small with so many large bodies in residence.

"I should have thought of it," Baal said. "I should have figured it out by the state of the carriage. We were attacked by flying scorpions after the Black Moon Ball … I should have figured it out."

"Orin planted evidence to suggest otherwise," Erebus said. "Do not blame yourself. We all believed Kai to be responsible."

"And now Orin will get what he wants." Baal's jaw was tight. "The hoard will grow in strength. The longer Kenna is missing, the more the realm descends into chaos. I can't believe we thought the hoard had been our protection against Orin and The Hunt, when all the time this thing had merely been gathering its strength by feeding off the hoard." He exhaled sharply. "We have to find her, but I doubt Orin will have her in his regular cells."

"There are rumours of catacombs under the city," Lauren said. "But as of yet the black mages have been unsuccessful in finding an entrance."

"Then we go in force," Erebus said. "We storm the palace, kill anyone who gets in our path, and search until we find her."

"And that could be exactly what they want us to do," Davin said. "Send forces after Kenna and leave the realm unguarded."

Baal squeezed his eyes closed. "We need to act. Do something now!"

This was the cool composed djinn that nothing seemed to faze? He was unravelling before Brett's eyes.

"Sabriel! Sabriel!" Baal circled the room. "Where the fuck is that angel? He knows where she is. He has to."

"Yes, but you know he cannot intervene," Erebus said.

Baal turned on him, green eyes practically shooting sparks. "I have ways to make even angels bleed."

Davin stepped forward and placed a hand on Baal's shoulder. "Calm, my friend. If we are to find her, we will need your logical mind to do so."

Baal took a shuddering breath. "We go under the palace. We use the sewers. Just a small group of us. We search."

It was a lame plan, but it was all they had.

The air behind Baal shimmered and Sabriel appeared. His blue eyes were dark and haunted. "I can't find her. I can't find her anywhere."

"Would you tell us even if you did?" Davin asked.

Sabriel buried his face in his hands. "It's my duty to watch over her, to be by her side in times of crisis and to comfort her. I was trusted to guide her."

"Why can't you find her?" Erebus asked. "You've never seemed to have problems before."

"There is a barrier between us. Something is tainting out connection." He looked up suddenly, his eyes widening. "Wait … I hear her."

Baal grabbed hold of the angel's tunic. "Where? Where is she?"

Sabriel locked eyes with Baal. "I … I can't."

Baal punched him in the face. There was no blood. In fact, Sabriel didn't even flinch. He stared at Baal with an expression of awe, and what looked like dawning comprehension.

"This was the way it was always meant to be," the angel said.

"What the fuck are you talking about?" Baal shook him by the lapels. "Sabriel are you unhinged?"

"No." Sabriel smiled. "But I do believe that for a time I may have been. You will find Kenna where you thought her to be. But she is deep underground. That is all I can tell you."

"Get her out!" Baal said. "Do it now. I know you can."

"Just because I can, it does not mean that I should. I am an angel, and my purpose it to watch. Not intervene."

He said it as if he was reminding himself of the fact.

Brett was done listening to this bullshit. "There has to be something else you can do."

"Yes. I will stay with her. Comfort her until help arrives." He looked too Baal, whose fists were still tangled in the fabric of his tunic. "You will save her. It is your destiny to be together, and I have faith that nothing will come between you this time." He vanished

Baal stared at the spot where the angel had been. "This time? What the fuck?"

"We should leave now," Erebus said. "If we ride nonstop, we can make it to Twilight by tomorrow morning. We will search as long as it takes. The catacombs are real, and together we will find them."

It would have been a rousing speech if it hadn't been for the fact that they all knew this search could take days, weeks even. By that time, it might be too late for Kenna. Brett doubted Orin had taken her as a hostage. He'd taken her as a prize for Legion. He would feed her to it. There was no time. And yet they all moved to the door, intent on doing the only thing they could.

"Wait." Davin's command was soft, but it cut through the air like a knife. "I can find her."

"What?" Baal turned to him, incredulous. "How? And why not tell us sooner?"

Davin bowed his head. "I've been running and hiding all my life. And if it were anyone else I would keep my lips sealed and continue hiding, but I cannot let Kenna perish to save my own hide."

He stepped away from them and tucked in his chin, the air shimmered and a flash of amber light filled the room. When it cleared, the Davin that stood before them was something entirely new. His hair shimmered gold and green, and huge iridescent emerald wings rose up from his back.

"What is this?" Erebus's hand was on the hilt of his sword.

Davin held up a hand. "My true form. I'm an abomination. My mother was a djinn and my father and angel. If the angels find me, they will unmake me, so I hide."

Brett winced. "You're not hiding now."

"Yes, because this is the only way to find her. I have the same abilities as Sabriel. I can go to her. I may not be able to track her like her guardian angel, but now that he knows where she is, I can tune in to the angel frequency and find her that way. But once I do that, there won't be much time. They will sense me, hone in on me, and come for me. I will get her back to you, and then I must leave."

Baal nodded. "Bring her back and we will petition the angels to allow you to remain among us as the honourable djinn you have proven yourself to be."

Davin smiled wryly. "That is kind of you, but there is no need. I believe that this is to be my fate, and I accept it. The few weeks I have had here have been the happiest of my life. Please tell Kenna that it was an honour to have known her."

He closed his eyes and vanished.

"So what now?" Lauren asked.

Baal fell back into the nearest seat, his face pale. "Now we wait."

22

My head rang from the blows the guard had rained down on me. I'd laughed in his face, taking the hits like a fucking trooper. Yeah, he was pissed—pissed that they'd lost some leverage. But that made Mum's death count for something.

A shudder ran through me. I wanted to raise my head and check out the black shit's progress through my veins, but my limbs had gone into shut-down again. How many times had he injected me now? Three? No, this was the fourth round. Round and round the merry-go-round. Sabriel. I needed my angel. He could hold my hand, couldn't he? Where was he? Why wasn't he here? Had he forsaken me? Forsaken, ha! Listen to me with my fancy words. Impeding death was turning me into a scholar. Or was it poking holes in my mind to mimic Swiss cheese. Wait. The cell was being sucked away.

"Kenna? Kenna hold on."

Sabriel? My heart lurched with hope, but the cell was gone and I was back in the cavern again.

There was no time to dwell, I needed to act fast and burn the shit out of the taint inside me before Legion grabbed me. I'd done it three times. I could do it again, right? Except this time, when I reached for the flame, it didn't flare to life enthusiastically. In fact, it was barely a flicker. Oh god, had I used it all up? Was that even possible? Maybe it needed time to recharge? Orin's guard wasn't giving me time to recharge!

The shadows on the cavern began to lengthen, moving toward me. Behind them was the maw, waiting to devour me. It was coming, getting closer— too close. Come on, please. Squeezing my eyes shut, I focused on the power inside me, channelling everything I had left into that flickering tired flame. Just one more burn, please. I needed time. Just a little more time.

Icy breath caressed the nape of my neck, and a low chuckle reverberated around the stone chamber.

"Not long now little pig. Soon you will belong to Legion."

My bowels went fluid just as the flame surged up to do its thing. I opened my eyes, back in the cell to find Sabriel looking down on me.

I winced and attempted to sit up. "What took you so long?"

Sabriel's eyes glistened with tears. "I couldn't find you. I tried and tried, but I couldn't find you, and then you called to me."

"If I'd known that was all I needed to do…" A cough wracked my body and something wet crawled up my throat, filled my mouth. I wiped at it, my hands coming away crimson.

"You're bleeding," Sabriel said.

"I'm dying."

"No." He shook his head, pulling me into his lap and cradling me. "I won't let you."

"You can't interfere, remember?"

He made a sound in his throat, part laugh and part pain. "For the first time in my existence, I truly hate what I am. What I have become."

I sighed into his shirt. "You lied about Baal, didn't you?"

He rested his chin on my head. "Yes."

I exhaled in relief. My heart hadn't steered me wrong. I wanted to be mad at Sabriel, but I needed him. Soon the guard would return with the final dose that would conquer me. I was out of juice. If they injected me again it was over, Legion would have me. But I needed to know, to understand, why my friend had tried to break my heart.

"Why did you do it?"

His chest rumbled in a sigh. "Because I love you."

I raised my head to look into his azure eyes and he reached up to push the damp tendrils of hair off my face.

"I've loved you forever Kenna. I loved you when you were Dante and I love you now."

What? "What did you say?"

His smile was filled with sorrow. "Another rule broken."

"Sabriel? What did you mean you loved me when I was Dante?"

"Your soul has been through many incarnations, and one of the first was Dante."

This should be shocking news, so why did it feel right? "I was Dante."

"And now you are Kenna. You are entirely you, but your soul lived in a different body once, and those memories are there somewhere, just not accessible to you. You were Dante once, and you were formidable—a true warrior."

"What really happened?"

"I was tasked to watch over you, and I was intrigued. Why send an angel to watch over a djinn? But angels do not question the creator, and so I did my duty, until it became a duty no more. I fell in love with her, with the you of the past. And for the first time an angel felt envy, jealousy, and the urge to lie. It was I who left clues to convince Baal that Dante was having an affair with Erebus. On the day that she died, she'd been with Erebus, yes. She'd lied to Baal about her whereabouts, yes, but only because they'd been searching for the perfect wedding present for Baal."

"You made Baal believe Dante was on a tryst with Erebus?"

He tucked in his chin, and closed his eyes. "Yes."

I swallowed the bitter bile rising up in my throat. "Go on."

"Baal was on the cliff side when Dante found him. He'd been upset, thinking of how to confront her. There was an altercation and Dante slipped and fell to her death."

"So it was an accident."

"Yes. Baal discovered the gift in her dresser a few days later, with a love note addressed to him. He realised his suspicions had been unfounded, that Dante had truly loved him."

But it was too late. She was gone.

"You were gone," Sabriel said echoing my thoughts. "They punished me for my transgression, but not as harshly as I punished myself, and then they gave me you to watch over. I knew who you were as soon as I laid eyes on you, and it was as if my heart came back to life. But I was adamant not to make the same mistake again."

"But you did."

He nodded. "When you told me you loved Baal, something inside me snapped. It was as if something else took over, and words, horrible lies, came spilling from my lips. I wanted to bite them back, but at the same time I wanted to see where they led." He leaned his forehead against mine. "This is where they led. If I hadn't placed doubts in your mind toward Baal, he would have been with you in that carriage. He would have saved you."

Where was my anger? The tirade toward him for betraying my trust? It seemed the fire had taken my rage with it.

"It's too late now." I pressed my hand to his chest and pulled back. "You can't interfere, but you can deliver a message."

He blinked back tears and nodded.

So I told him everything I'd learned. "You need to let them know what they're dealing with. You need to tell Baal to find a way to kill it. Tell him … tell him I love him."

Sabriel pressed his lips together. "I won't need to. They're on their way. They know Orin has you. Your friend Brett has been having dreams. He told Baal … your conclusions are the same. And Brett may have a solution, a way to end Legion."

So they were on their way. Hope was a fickle thing, deserting you one moment and holding your hand the next. I shrugged it off. It was unlikely they'd find me in time. Not without Sabriel leading them to me, which was something he couldn't do.

The key scraped in the lock.

The guard was back.

My time was up.

23

This time there was no messing about, no creepy I'm-gonna-get-you approach. This time Legion grabbed me by the throat and dug in its claws. This time I looked into its eyes, so many fucking eyes staring back at me, into me, pulling me apart into tiny pieces of myself and reorganising my essence into neat compartmentalised parts. Here was the piece that loved my friends, the part that was loyal to my cause. Here was the element that loved donuts and anything loaded with sugar. Here was that naughty sex drive, and the deeply buried component that yearned to be whole, that wanted a flesh and bone leg to stand on. Legion was taking me apart, and there was nothing I could do but sob silently as it claimed my mind.

Please …

Who was I imploring?

I was inside Legion, being sucked down and fragmenting as I went. They were hungry for me, eager to know me.

"Kenna, come back to me," Sabriel's voice latched onto me like a hook in the back of my skull. "Come back to me." The downward motion halted, and I began to rise.

"Yes, that's it. Come back."

The gloom was below me now, still reaching for me, but I was moving too fast out of its reach. Sabriel was doing something, goodness knows what, but he was saving me. And then something latched onto my ankle. Cold and uncompromising, I jerked in place, suspended between Sabriel's pull and Legions tug.

No. I wasn't going down there. I kicked out, swaying in place. The abyss echoed with my screams of rage.

"Get off! Get off me now you fucker!"

"No, no, no," Sabriel's sobs joined my cries. "I won't. I won't let you go."

Heat bloomed in my chest, spreading outward, eating away at the black goop inside my veins. This wasn't fire, this was something else, something familiar yet alien. Legion's grip on my ankle loosened and I kicked out again, and again. The warmth filled me and wrapped around me like a loving embrace. I was flying. My heart was soaring, and there was light raining down on me from above. I lifted my chin and felt it caress my face with loving fingers.

"Home, Kenna, come home."

I opened my eyes on a gasp. Sabriel's face was a beatific vision. His smile emanated love. A single tear slid down his cheek and his lips moved, mouthing the words: I love you. And then he shattered into a billion motes of light.

"Kenna, you're all right. You're safe."

"Davin?" How was this happening? Why did he have wings? I was dead. That's what this was. I was dead and this was all an illusion, a trick of my dying mind.

"You're safe."

His arms were pretty solid for an illusion, and his hair against my cheek felt real enough. "This is real?"

He pressed his lips to my forehead. "Yes, Kenna, this is real."

The cell was filled with light rising off his shoulders, and glowing from his wings. I'd never seen Sabriel's wings …

"Where did Sabriel go?" I knew. Deep down I knew, but I needed to hear Davin say it.

"Home. He is at one with the creator now. He gifted you his angel light, his divinity. He saved you, and he will forever be a part of you. But you will not see him again."

A sob caught in my throat. "He's dead."

"Nothing ever really dies. But we have no more time left. We must leave this place now." He clasped me tighter. "Close your eyes."

Leave, yes. I needed to leave, but there was someone I had to take with me. "Mum, we have to take Mum."

Davin glanced down at the twisted mutated body of my mother. "She is already home, Kenna. Her soul is at peace. That is merely a shell. Close your eyes."

And then we were stepping into a dazzling portal of light and it was impossible to see.

24

"Kenna? Can you hear me?"

I opened my eyes and stared up into Baal's beloved face. His jade eyes roved over me, his brow furrowed in concern. The tightness around his eyes and mouth spoke a thousand words. I reached up and touched his lips.

"I can hear you."

An exhale exploded from his lips, and then I was hauled up against his chest. He buried his hands in my hair and pressed his lips on mine. He kissed me as if I was the last breath of air and the last drop of moisture on an arid planet. My eyes burned and my throat tightened as the sobs I'd held back pressed against the back of my nose.

I'd thought I was going to die, that I'd never see him again. Never get to tell him how much I loved him. I kissed him like it was my last moment on earth, which it almost had been, and then I pulled back and locked gazes with him. He blinked back tears, but I didn't bother. I let mine fall. And then we were laughing—totally inappropriate, relieved, crazy laughter.

Someone coughed.

I looked up, noticing the other occupants of the room for the first time. Erebus, Lauren, Brett, and Irina were looking at me strangely, almost warily. And what was that in Irina's hand? It looked like a tattoo gun. I noted the burning in my left hand for the first time. Shit, it was covered in black ink—swirls and whorls—and beneath it, barely visible, was the pulse and shift of black veins.

"Oh, god! It's still inside me!" I flapped my arm desperate to shake it off.

"It's okay," Baal pressed me back into my seat. "We have it contained, and once your flame has recharged you can burn it out of your system. It seems that even Sabriel's angel fire wasn't enough to cleanse your body."

Okay, I could handle this. It was contained, beneath a web of enchanted ink. I swung my legs off the chaise. "Where's Davin?"

Baal shook his head. "He had to leave. I'll explain later, but right now you need to tell us what happened to you. Davin told us about the taint, he found Sabriel trying to revive you. You were dead," Baal swallowed, his eyes darkening. "Or so it seemed."

Legion had taken me then, but Sabriel had pulled me back. The story fell from my lips with ease, but then I got to the part where I'd had to kill Mum, and I faltered.

"It's all right," Brett said. "You did what she wanted. You saved her."

I nodded, and wiped at my running nose. Was I crying again? Damn this shit. Damn Legion for taking my mother, and my friend, and countless others. We had to end this. Baal offered me his handkerchief.

"Thanks." I blew my nose. "But there's more. Mum told me about Orin, she told me he's my grandfather."

The room was deathly silent.

"The birthmark on his face..." Brett said. "I saw it, or at least I thought I did but then I convinced myself it was an illusion."

"But that makes you the only surviving heir to the Twilight throne," Baal said.

"Right now I don't give a damn about that. I just need to stop Legion." I continued skimming over the conversation with Sabriel, my stomach turning because I'd have to tell Baal soon, how I'd doubted him and how … how I was Dante, or had been. I was still trying to wrap my head around that one. I finished to a hush.

"We have to find a way to stop it," I met Erebus's gaze, then Brett's. "We have to kill it."

"I dreamed of The Hunt," Brett said. "Long story, but basically they told me that only harmony of the races could kill it. They'd managed to weaken it and trap it using the blood of the ocean people. It took wiping out a race to push it back into the abyss. And the ascendants of the ocean people died from grief at the loss of their children."

"Wait," Erebus said. "They're not all dead." He looked to me. "We have Adamaris back at the fortress in Evernight. He's still in the pool in the garden."

I pressed my lips together. "We're not killing him to take his blood, besides I doubt it would help much."

Erebus snorted. "No, it would hardly be a harmonic action. But he may know another way to weaken Legion. He is old, ancient. He must have been here when this thing landed in our world."

It was a long shot, but it was all we had, because being on the verge of attack wasn't really conducive to harmony.

I met Erebus's silver gaze. "How bad is the hoard?"

"It's stirring and beginning to awaken. I must return to Evernight soon. The others will need my assistance."

We didn't say it, but the unspoken comment was there—maybe we should have held off on severing our tether. But even if we hadn't, with the state I was in I'd have been little help to Erebus and his clan.

"Are you taking the dark djinn with you?"

"A few warriors. The rest will remain here, at your disposal."

"No. I'm coming with you. Baal can hold the fort in my absence. I need to speak with Adamaris."

"And how will you do that?" Lauren said. "I heard tales of the oceanic folk while growing up, I'm not sure how much is myth and how much fact, but the consensus is they cannot communicate above water."

Yes, Adamaris had struggled to speak to me above water, but he'd spoken to me fine when I'd been under it. "Irina, is there a way to allow me to speak underwater, to breathe, even if it is for a short time?"

Irina nodded. "Yes, I think there may be. I'll just need to gather some herbs. It will take a couple of hours to steep."

I looked to Erebus. "You good to wait?"

He nodded.

"Lauren," I smiled at my friend. "I need you to keep an eye on Orin and let us know as soon as he is mobilising his forces."

"I'll page Baal as soon as anything happens."

"My troops are in place," Baal said. "Camped out on the borders of the realm. The Overlords have been informed of your safe return and an announcement made to the public, but until they see you, I doubt they will believe it. I'm hoping Kai will be generous enough to spread the word, after all it was your return that led to his release."

So, Orin's plan to throw them off the scent had worked.

Baal sighed. "In the meantime, we need to get you washed and fed." He scooped me up into his arms and strode toward the exit.

I opened my mouth to protest but snapped it closed again. He was right, I reeked, plus my gut told me that things were about to get ugly out there and this may be my last down moment before the world went to shit.

I'd take what I could get.

***

The water was hot, but not scalding. I lay beneath the suds, allowing Baal to massage my scalp and scrub away the aches and pains. Davin was gone. He'd exposed his secret to save me and was now on the run. When this was over we'd have to do something about his predicament. No one had the right to unmake him for being who he was—an amazing individual. Baal left me to soak a moment, and the steam, the hugging heat, leaded my lids until I couldn't keep them open any longer.

The world tilted and I was standing by the tub looking down on myself sleeping. My head was tipped back, arms gripping the side of the tub. I could reach out right now and place the palm of my hand on my bathing self's head. It wouldn't take much to hold her down. She'd flail and fight, but soon the water would enter her lungs and she'd drown. Then the vessel would be mine.

The vessel.

I raised my arm and stared at the black veins throbbing beneath my pretty human skin. I glared at the ink holding me prisoner. Home wasn't far. I could take this vessel home. But she would fight me. She was strong. But Legion was patient and it was almost time for us to rise. Still, it would be fun to watch her flail.

I reached, palm out, and touched her silver head.

I awoke on a gasp, my hand shooting out to smack away the hand reaching for me.

"It's all right," Baal said. "You were dreaming."

Dreaming? I stared at my black inked hand. Had it been a dream?

"Kenna? Are you all right."

He lifted me out. I was pink and clean, but the lethargy that should have infused my limbs was absent. Baal wrapped me in the hugest fluffiest towel I'd ever seen, and lay me on the bed before lowering himself down beside me.

His gaze travelled over my face and his fingers made lazy circles on my bare shoulder, soothing away the final dregs of the vision, dream, whatever it had been.

"I'm sorry I wasn't there to protect you," he said softly. "I should have insisted on coming with you."

"I would have insisted you didn't." I sighed and closed my eyes, a sick feeling blooming in my stomach, because if we were going to move forward then he needed to know the truth. He needed to know that I'd doubted him. He needed to know I would never doubt him again.

"The reason I asked you not to come with me, the reason I was weird with you for the last couple of days, was because someone told me something about you, something bad, and I allowed myself to believe it."

His fingers froze on my shoulder and his eyes narrowed. "Who was it?"

"Sabriel."

His emerald eyes clouded in confusion. "What did he say?"

I told him everything—about Sabriel's accusations, about my denial, and then reluctant acceptance. I told him about Mum's revelation in the carriage and how Sabriel had confessed at the end, but I didn't tell him about Dante ... that I was her, or had been. I needed him to forgive me for me, not for who I'd been.

I pressed my hand to his chest. "So you see, I doubted you. I doubted my feelings and my instincts and that is what caused this. I'm sorry, so sorry. Can you ever forgive me?"

His expression was stony. My eyes pricked and I pressed my lips together.

Baal slipped off the bed. "Get dressed, Kenna. I want to show you something."

He kept his gaze averted while I pulled on my prosthetic and quickly dressed. He hated me. Great. I should have just kept my big mouth shut. But if I'd done that, my guilt would have eaten away at me. No. I'd done the right thing, and if he didn't forgive me then ... then I'd have to deal with it.

"I'm ready."

Baal walked onto the balcony and held out his arms to me. "Come."

If this was the last time he was going to hold me then I'd make the most of the contact. The air kicked up around us and we were flying. I held on tight, inhaling his scent, that liquorice aroma that made my heart ache with longing. We landed on soft grass a moment later in a part of the grounds I didn't recognise. A tall hedgerow grew to our left.

"Where are we?"

Baal released me and walked off parallel to the hedge. "Come, Kenna."

I followed, the grass soft and cushioning beneath my boots. Baal stopped by a tangle of ivy, leaned in and vanished.

What the heck?

I rushed forward and stopped by the ivy plant. Shit, where had he gone? "Baal?"

A hand shot out from the ivy, grabbed my wrist and yanked me forward. I tumbled through the green into a sun soaked garden. Fountains, a gazebo, a huge lounge swing and flowers—hundreds of pink and purple blooms—Dante's favourite flower. The scent hit me then, so strong it made my head reel.

I walked up to the fountain filled with crystal clear water. "It's beautiful."

"It was our place, Dante's and mine. We found it on one of our trysts and claimed it. We'd meet here often and spend lazy days under the sun. The polyander flower was her favourite, so I planted them here for her." He locked gazes with me. "I would never have hurt her. Yes, I thought she might have been having an affair with Erebus, and it killed me, but my plan was to let her go. I wanted her to be happy." His jaw tensed. "I was ready to forgive her, but Sabriel I doubt I would have been so forgiving with. He planted lies, he is the reason she is dead. I never got to tell her how sorry I was, or beg her forgiveness for doubting her. She would never have doubted me like that. I've carried that guilt for decades."

"I think she knows." It was clear now, the strange connection we had. The aroma only I could smell when around him. It was a memory. Dante had associated this place with him, the scent of the blooms with him.

"Kenna?" He took a step toward me. "I want you to know that I understand how doubts can be sown. I understand because I too have been a victim. My doubt killed your sister."

"Nothing ever truly dies." I smiled recalling Davin's words. "And neither did Dante."

His brow furrowed. "What? What do you mean?"

I pressed my hand to my breastbone. "She lives on in me. In my soul."

His brow cleared. "What are you saying?"

"Sabriel told me … He told me I was Dante."

He took another step toward me and I held up my hand. "But I'm not now. You get that right? I'm me. I'm Kenna."

Baal bridged the gap between us and tilted my chin with the crook of his finger. "Listen to me, Kenna. Look into my eyes, into my heart, and hear me. I loved Dante, but she died. She died, and I grieved, and I moved on. Then I met you and felt things I'd never believed possible. I loved Dante, but I am in love with you Kenna. Heart rending, can't-breathe-without-you love. Forever love." His lips lifted in a crooked smile.

There were no words, because he'd said it all. I wrapped my hand around the back of his neck and pushed up on my tiptoes to press my lips to his. I kissed him softly, teasingly. His fingers tightened on my waist, digging in. He was holding back, letting me take the lead when all he wanted to do was throw me down and take me. My pulse kicked up. I needed him to lose control. To take the lead. Pressing my body against his, I flicked out my tongue and swept it over his bottom lip before drawing it into my mouth. A low moan shook his chest, and then I was hauled up against him, his hands in my hair, his mouth devouring mine. He lifted me off my feet and onto the ground.

Thank goodness for soft grass.

***

I found Brett and Irina holed up in my study. Erebus had recruited five dark djinn and was ready to go. Baal was running damage control with the other Overlords after Kai had gone whining about being unjustly tortured.

Brett hugged me, careful not to accidentally crush. "I'm coming with," he said.

"To Evernight?"

"Yes. I spoke to Erebus. I'm on the hoard watch crew." He grinned, showcasing glinting diamond teeth.

"I have the potion," Irina held up the vial. "You'll get about five minutes of underwater time with this. You won't need to breath, and you'll be able to project your thoughts."

I reached for the potion and she snatched it away. "No. I'm coming with you. Erebus told me what happened last time you got close to the water creature Adamaris. I'm going to make sure that doesn't happen again."

She had a point. "Fine. Any progress with the serum?"

Irina glanced at Brett, who crossed his arms over his chest.

"What's going on?"

Irina pulled out another vial. "The serum is ready, but Brett won't take it."

"Brett? What the heck?"

"I'll take it when this is over. Right now I'm more use to you like this."

"Do you think I give a damn about how useful you can be? You need to take the damn serum and get back to being you."

Brett stood, his huge frame towering over me. "What I need to do is be in shape to kick some fucking ass. Caldwell is confidant the serum will work, but it may knock me out completely, or leave me weak. I can't take the risk. Lindrealm could be attacked at any moment."

He had a point. I'd probably be make the same decision. "Fine. But as soon as this is over, you take it, 'kay?"

"Yes, boss."

I grinned. "It's your majesty now, I got an upgrade."

He chuckled. "Fine. Your majesty."

Irina's gaze was fixed on my inked hand. "How are you feeling?" she asked.

"Okay." I raised my hand and turned it over. "The tattoos are working."

She nodded. "Good. It's an ancient runic barrier spell. Are you strong enough to burn it out yet?"

"Probably, but I don't want to risk burning out. Like Brett said, Lindrealm could be attacked at any moment. If I use my flame for this, it could leave me weakened."

There was a rap on the door and Erebus stepped in. "We're ready to leave."

My hand went to Frieda, snug at my waist. Baal had retrieved her from the carriage wreckage.

"Let's get this over with."

***

Erebus took the reins as I settled on the leoequise. We were in motion almost immediately. Brett, due to his size, had opted to ride with Irina, and they'd taken the largest of the mounts. Once out of the palace gates, we picked up speed, galloping away from the Black Forest to the east and toward the Cinder lands to the west. Evernight lay beyond the arid landscape, half a day's ride if we rode nonstop, which was what we'd planned to do.

I patted the mount. "Don't these creatures ever get tired?"

"The leoequise are hardy beasts," Erebus said. "They need very little food or water, and are able to ride long distances without breaks. They make the perfect mount for long journeys and battles, but their numbers are dwindling."

"Why?"

"Not enough young are born, and the few that are birthed die young. This pack is the last of its kind, and so far they've shown no interest in procreation."

We rode in silence for the next hour or so, past markets and homes and taverns and down winding dirt tracks and across open fields. The fifth dimension was truly beautiful, and when this was over, I'd take a tour and enjoy every part of it to the fullest.

I relaxed against him. "When did you last get word from Aidan, Baron, and Vale?"

"An hour ago."

"While we were riding?"

"Yes."

I had to know. "What are they?"

"They are my clan."

"Yeah, but what does that mean? I thought you were the only dark djinn left when the others disappeared. So where did Aiden, Baron, Samson, and Vale come from? In fact, surely you've wondered why The Hunt didn't take you too?"

"I've wondered, yes."

I waited for him to continue. The lush green gave way to hard packed earth. Up ahead the sky was purple, and even further in the distance it took on an indigo hue that reminded me of Baal's hair.

"We approach the Cinder lands," Erebus said. "Hold fast, we will ride like the wind. The Cinder lands are not a place to stop."

It looked like the conversation was over.

The leoequise let out a rumbling cry, and then we were moving so fast. I was forced to close my eyes against the hot wind in my face.

Putting my questions about Erebus's clan aside, I focused on the task ahead of me. The thought of climbing into the lake with Adamaris didn't tickle me, but it had to be done.

Hopefully, when this was over, I'd have the answers we needed to defeat Legion.

25

BRETT

So, this was the hoard—this mass of inky viscous darkness slowly bubbling toward the gate. It was less than a quarter of a mile away from them and creeping across the ground like an obsidian mist. Denizens burst from their Evernight burrows, skittering and sliding away from the destructive masse's path. The ones that got trapped in it turned on each other in a fight to the death.

"How long before it reaches us?" Brett asked Erebus.

"Not long."

"It began to move when Kenna was taken," the dark djinn called Aidan said. "We were hoping that now she's been found it would settle again, that the relief of the masses would leech away the hoard's strength."

"It may still settle," Baron said. "I believe it is slowing down."

It was too hard to tell. But this was what they did, they watched the hoard and they kept it at bay, so he'd take their word on it.

Erebus walked over to the dark djinn that had travelled with him from the fifth dimension. They began to speak in their strange guttural tongue. Something to the left of the hoard, probably a hundred metres or so, caught Brett's eye. It looked like mist, no, a dust cloud.

"What's that?" He pointed out the phenomenon.

Vale followed his gaze. "Erebus, we have incoming."

"What is it?" Brett pressed.

Erebus broke away from his people and drew his sword.

The dust cloud was advancing rapidly, overtaking the hoard, and shit, it was no dust cloud, it was a hoard of a different kind—a bloody denizen stampede.

"Ready yourselves." Erebus took up station beside Brett.

Brett drew his everlight blade, the luma gleaming wickedly in the darkness. A surge of adrenaline, warm and familiar, rushed through what remained of his human veins. This was what he'd been born to do. Finally, something he could kick the shit out of.

The denizen hoard attacked, desperate to get through the gate, and with an earth-shattering roar Brett countered.

Blood, thick and black and bitter, flesh torn and bloody and warm. Here in Evernight, the denizens didn't fold in on themselves and blink out of existence. Here in Evernight you got to eviscerate the fuckers.

"Hold the line," Aidan bellowed.

"There are more," Vale shouted. "Coming from the west."

Sure enough, another cloud was advancing on them.

"What fuck is going on?" Erebus sliced the head off a creeper.

Brett took out the legs on a scuttler. "This doesn't happen often?"

"This never happens," Erebus said. "Something has them spooked."

"The hoard?"

"No, it's more than that."

A loud buzz, like the rotors on a helicopter, filled the air. The denizens faltered in their attack and went impossibly still.

"What the ..."

It was coming from above, above and all around. The moon went out for a moment, obscured by a dark cloud ... a rapidly moving dark cloud. The denizens were silent now, silent and frozen, as if waiting instruction.

"Erebus? What the heck is that?"

Erebus stared at the mass in the sky, his mouth slightly agape, and his silver eyes wide with astonishment.

"Erebus!"

Denizens. Hybrid denizens.

Brett's pulse skipped a beat. "They're headed for the gate."

Erebus locked gazes with him. "It's happening. It's happening now."

He had to warn them. Had to enforce curfew and get the Fearless on the streets. And the way back was right behind him.

Brett took a stumbling step backward. "Get Kenna, tell her what's happening. I have to go." He turned and ran full pelt for the gate.

"Brett, wait!"

But there was no time. Lindrealm was about to be under attack, and he needed to be on the front lines when it happened.

<u>26</u>

Erebus had dropped us off at the fortress, then run off to join Vale, Aiden, and Baron at the gate. Brett had gone with him. There was nothing he could do in Lindrealm right now, not until Orin attacked. But the hoard was something he could help keep at bay. Lauren was probably in Twilight by now, with his finger on the pulse, and Irina was by my side. Her mouth parted slightly in awe as we stepped through the doors into the fortress. It greeted me, as it had the last time, sending warm welcoming vibes to envelope me.

"What was that?" Irina said.

"You felt it?"

"I felt … something."

"It's the fortress saying hi." I walked toward the nearest door. I could make my way through the vast structure and find the courtyard, but it was easier for the fortress to take us straight to it. Visualising the garden, I pushed open the door, and stepped out into the night air.

"How?" Irina glanced back to see the courtyard doors, wide open doors that led into a marbled seating area.

"It's magic, Irina." I grinned. "You should know all about that."

She swallowed and nodded. "Of course. Enchanted."

The garden was just as I remembered it, tranquil and beautiful in the midst of the deadly Evernight. I led Irina down the pathway bordered by the gorgeous white moonflowers and toward the pool where Adamaris resided. It gleamed in the lunar light, smooth and serene. Erebus had admonished him for trying to drown me, but that hadn't been what he'd been doing. He'd tried to speak to me, and now I had the means to listen and speak back.

"Remember," Irina said. "You only have five or six minutes at the most."

We came to a standstill by the pool's edge, and she tied the rope securely around my waist. "I'll pull you up in five minutes, if you start to feel like the potion is wearing off sooner, just tug on the rope and I'll pull you straight out."

"Gotcha. Let's do this."

She handed me the vial containing the gloopy, vile-looking concoction.

I took it gingerly. "This is gonna taste bad, isn't it?"

"Yes. I'm afraid so."

Thumbing off the stopper and exhaling through my nose, I downed the contents, swallowing quickly. It was bitter, and the stench was … I gagged and slapped a hand over my mouth to stop myself spewing. Breathe, slow and easy. Ice-cream and chocolate, that's what it was. Nice tasty stuff …

The urge to puke subsided. "Is it working?"

"Only one way to find out." Irina indicated the pool.

Time to take a dip. The water was cold, but not icy. Best to just jump right in. With a final look over my shoulder at Irina, I did just that. The water closed over my head, and I opened my eyes to the murky gloom below. Adamaris was probably hiding further down. Kicking out, I pushed myself toward the depths. How did this work? Could I call out to him? Irina had said the potion would amplify my thoughts. I'd be able to project them and receive his. Okay.

Okay, time to get thinking. "Adamaris. You here? I need to speak with you."

The water was getting darker, and the sense of being trapped grew stronger. The urge to turn and swim back to the surface gripped my chest in a vice. No. I'd come this far, there was no way I'd leave without answers.

"Adamaris!"

The gloom below shifted, and he appeared below me, his huge dark eyes comically wide.

"You came back." His mouth didn't move, but his words were in my head. He swam up to join me, circling me. "Erebus was angry."

"He thought you were trying to kill me."

"No. I was trying to warn you."

"Warn me? About what?"

"About the binding and the flame, that others had come before you and been bound. They'd died."

"Yeah, I found that out the hard way."

"But you did not die. You are here."

"Yes. Turns out I'm special."

His cocked his bald head. "Yes, yes, I believe you are."

He inched forward and reached up to cup my face. His fingers were strangely dry against my skin, considering we were submerged.

"I see it now. Oh, Kenna. I see it all." He released me. "I have wondered why grief did not take me. I wondered why I was spared even though I begged to be gone like my brethren."

"The grief of the ocean creatures after your land offspring died?"

"Yes."

"That's why I'm here. Legion—the thing your children's blood weakened—is rising. We need to know how to stop it. The Hunt says we must use the harmony of races, so I guess peace will put it to sleep, but that's kind of impossible when it's using Orin to attack us and cause chaos and fear. There has to be another way to kill it."

He moved in close, his green eyes glowing in the gloom. "Legion cannot be killed. Only the harmony of races can expel it from this world."

"No. I want to kill it, there has to be a way."

"No. Nothing ever truly dies, Kenna, it just changes form and moves on to another plane of existence. My people's lives here ended, but their journey continued elsewhere. But Legion knows only one form, and that is destruction."

"So, what? You're saying there's nothing we can do? That this is it? That we lose, and it wins?"

"I wondered why I did not die of grief, and now I know."

"Huh?" Why was he changing the subject.

He reached for me again. "My bloodline survived. One of my offspring escaped." He caressed my cheek.

"What are you talking about?"

"Ocean blood runs in your veins, it is weak, diluted by generations, but it is there. It is because you exist that I am still alive." He swam around me. "Have you any idea how lonely this existence is? How much I have longed for death?" He smiled, showcasing tiny razor-sharp teeth. "And now death is finally in my grasp."

What was he talking about? My chest began to burn. Oh shit. The potion was wearing off. I reached for the rope, ready to give it a tug and Adamaris lunged, grabbing me around the waist and pinning my arms to my side.

"What are you doing? Let me go."

"It's all right, Kenna. It will all be over in a moment. We will enter a beautiful dream, free and at peace."

Peace. He wanted to die, and if I was his last surviving descendant, then killing me would end him. He meant to kill me …

Oh god, I needed to breathe. "What if I'm not the last? What if there are others?"

He didn't falter in his grip. "I have to try."

Five minutes should be up. Come on Irina. The urge to take a breath was an inferno in my lungs. I couldn't take this much long—

My body jerked and Adamaris's grip loosened a fraction. Irina tugged again. Yes! I kicked out as Adamaris made a grab for me. My foot connected with his face, stunning him momentarily. It was the chance I needed. I kicked out again and used Irina's pull to propel myself upwards. Fingers grazed my ankle but failed to gain purchase, and then I was breaking the surface of the water.

"Dammit Kenna," Irina held out her hand to me. "What the heck—"

Adamaris surfaced and slammed into me. "No. No more life."

"Kenna!"

The rope around my waist tightened and I was ripped out of Adamaris's grip and pulled onto land.

I spat out water and pushed my wet hair off my face. "I fucking hate lakes."

Behind me Adamaris's wail of woe swelled to fill the night garden.

Irina helped me to my feet and away from the lake edge. "What happened?"

"He tried to kill me. Apparently, I'm a descendant. He thinks I'm the reason he's still here while the rest of his kind moved on to some other plane."

I turned to face him. "Adamaris, you fucking suck!"

He stared at me with his sparkling green eyes, as if a revelation had occurred to him. "Should tell you truth. Other way to be free. Harmony of races in you. All in you."

"What does he mean?" Irina asked.

"I have no idea, and there is no way I'm going back in there to find out." I untied the rope from my waist. "Let's get the hell out of here."

This whole trip had been a huge waste of time.

"Kenna!" Erebus appeared in courtyard ahead. "We have to leave now. Lindrealm is under attack."

***

The gate was a covered in denizens. They crawled and flew, slithered and scuttled. There was no sign of Vale, Aidan, or Baron. The other dark djinn were on the outskirts of the mass, hacking away at the surge. It was ineffectual, all pointless now, because the barrier had been breached and the monsters were in Lindrealm.

I grabbed Erebus's arm "I have to get through,"

He readied his sword. "And we will." He nodded at Irina and then locked gazes with me. "Are you ready?"

I drew Frieda and flicked my wrist to activate her, and tested my leg by pushing down with my knee and flexing. It was solid, smooth motion.

"I'm ready."

Irina drew her twin blades. "So am I."

I didn't ask her if she was sure, didn't tell her she needn't come with us. Lindrealm was in danger and we needed all the help we could get.

Erebus's battle cry reverberated through Evernight, and we charged. The night was replaced by a different kind of darkness as we plunged into the fray of squeals and hisses. The buzz from the airborne denizens filled my head, disorienting me for a moment, and then a black limb slammed into my shoulder, knocking me back a step. I lashed out with Frieda, cutting an arc through the denizen's bodies, back and forth, back and forth, making a path to the gate. Somewhere along the line I lost Irina and Erebus to the madness, but they'd make it through. Irina was a warrior mage in Baal's army, and Erebus ... well, he was Erebus.

The shimmering portal came into view, glimpses caught between the hairy, furry, bodies of the monsters of the night. Up above, the flying hybrids poured through the portal, vanishing into the mortal realm.

Almost there. Just a few metres more. I took out a scuttler to my left, disabling it by slicing off its legs. It fell to the ground, crushing a creeper with its huge mass. And then I was at the gate. The viscous surface shimmered and pulsed.

Something slammed into my back.

I was propelled through the gate head first.

27

BRETT

Everything was happening too fast. There was no time to set up, no time to prepare, only time to react. Brett manned the gate line—killing the fuckers as they came through. The Fearless at his back took up the slack. But the influx of denizens was too great. With regards to the airborne, there was only one line of defence. The pop and whirr of gunfire erupted around him as the regular enforcement officers took out the fliers using luma bullets—an ingenious new invention by Shamatech. Only problem was they'd had to use up their luma reserves making the damn bullets, and there weren't nearly enough. But the enforcement officers manning the mounted guns and the snipers stationed around the gate, were all expert marksman. The airborne winked out one by one as the bullets did their work.

He focused on the gate, on the creepers and scuttlers and all the new shit he'd never had the displeasure of dispatching before. At least when he killed them here they folded in and vanished. At least there'd be no bodies to dispose of when this was over.

He had to believe it would be over. That the invasion would come to an end and humanity would prevail.

"Brett, watch out!" Karl's shoulder slammed him into him, knocking him out of the way just in time to prevent him being impaled by a scorpion stinger. The appendage smashed into the ground, exactly where he'd been a moment ago, sending a cloud of cement dust flying up into the air.

Karl yelled and staggered back clutching his arm. Shit. He was hurt—torn shirt and blood tinged green. The stinger had grazed him on its downward arch. Poison, those things were poison. Brett dispatched the scorpion with a neat slice, lopping off its head, and then grabbed Karl's arm, pulling him to the side-lines of the battle.

"You need anti-venom. Now."

Karl gritted his teeth and fumbled in his cargo pants pocket. He pulled out a slender case, but his hands were shaking too much.

"Let me," Brett grabbed it, flipped it open, and retrieved the syringe.

He injected Karl in the neck. Someone screamed, a high-pitched sound followed by a gurgle. Brett turned in time to see a body, no, half a body flying through the air. Blood spattered his face as the Fearless torso sailed past him. It hit the ground with a wet thud.

Another Fearless down.

Another comrade lost.

Rage bubbled up inside him and a red haze descended on his vision. An inhuman roar exploded from his lips, shaking his chest and leaving his lungs aching. For a split second it was as if the world stood still. And then he was careening into the thick of it, into the midst of the carnage. Block, punch, slice, and twist—these fuckers had to die. There was nothing except the thunderous beat of his heart and the wet slice and pop of denizen death.

Time stood still as he dispatched the monsters, as his Fearless comrades ended those that managed to get past him, but the invasion kept coming. How many more were there? There were too many fallen Fearless, too many monsters to take on. All he could do was keep on killing. No sooner had he banished one, another took its place. He spun to face his next target. Its mouth was open, showcasing a spiral of deathly teeth descending into its gut. Brett froze for a fraction too long, mesmerised by the display of pink and white.

The jaws were almost on him. Shit. He brought Lance round, but the thing exploded in a spray of black before he could land a blow—the tiny pieces folding away to nothing. The mist dispersed, leaving Kenna standing before him, chest heaving and silver hair flying.

Her lips curved in a wicked smile. "Getting sloppy soldier. Need me to show you how it's done?"

He grinned, the knot in his chest loosening. He swept out a hand. "Be my guest."

Kenna dropped him a wink and then spun into action. He allowed himself a brief moment to admire her form, her balance, her thrusts and her jabs, and then he joined her. Back to back, side by side. Like the good old days. Yeah, Kenna Carter was fucking back.

The dynamic duo was back.

28

This felt good, this felt right. Being here with Brett, fighting beside him, I was my old self again, the Kenna that killed denizens for a living. Except this time the pay check would need to be ten times the usual size.

Erebus burst through the gate, followed closely by Irina and his clan. The dark djinn came through a moment later. With the djinn aid, the denizens began to fall rapidly. These warriors were beasts of a different kind, unrelenting, untiring. They sliced and dispatched so fast that my head span.

"We're doing it. The flow is slowing," Brett said

As if sensing our imminent victory, the Fearless let up a morale-boosting battle cry and surged toward the gate with renewed vigour. An answering rush of heat gripped my chest. And then the denizens faltered. We took out several before we realised they weren't actually fighting back. A low rumble shook the ground, and a low-level buzz filled the air. The hairs on the back of my neck stood to attention.

"Something's coming," Irina said. She turned her wrists, her blades glinting in the sunlight.

They burst through the gate like a fresh wave of death. Twice as large as the regular denizens and ten times as lethal—hybrid denizens. They cannibalised the regular denizens in an attempt to cut a path toward us. There were too many—hundreds against maybe thirty Fearless, half of which were wounded, running on their last puffs of steam. They came to a halt several metres from the gate, twitching and salivating as if awaiting further instruction.

And then Legion spoke—its voice emanating from every hybrid maw with cutting clarity. "Submit to me and no more will die."

My inked hand burned and stung, and the edges of my vision darkened until I was looking down a tunnel, travelling down it, fast. Too fast to see my surroundings, my momentum slowed, and black-leaved trees surrounded me, pulling me forward until a huge blackened trunk loomed over me. The tree was as wide as a house and covered in moss, but my journey didn't stop there, I was moving forward, toward the trunk, toward the moss. It was in my face, soft and inviting, sucking me in, into the tree. No. The illusion evaporated, my vision cleared, and I was back on the battlefield.

"Join me and all shall live." Legion continued. "There is no hope against my force. Become the force, and you all shall be spared."

What had just happened? What had I just seen? Now wasn't the time. I needed to focus. This was it. We were battered and tired and severely outnumbered. Legion had us by the balls, and he knew it. There was no way we were taking out these fuckers hand to hand. I was good, but even I had my limits.

"We need to fall back." I turned to Brett. "We need to fall back, take cover. If we stay out in the open, we'll die."

Brett nodded. "Fall back! Take cover."

The hybrids remained stationary. Maybe they saw our retreat as compliance. But like fuck was I giving Legion anything. If it was a choice between a clean death and becoming a soldier of darkness, I'd take a clean death any day. Yes, it was unfair not to offer Lindrealm a choice, unfair to make a decision for them, but if I allowed them to decide I knew they'd want to live, no matter the cost, because humanity … humanity coveted survival above all. If Legion got its claws into them, then the millions of djinn in the fifth dimension would be lost. If Legion took Lindrealm, these people were as good as dead anyway. There was only one course of action—a fight to the death. A sharp pang of regret had my eyes stinging. Baal … I wouldn't get to see him again.

Shaking off the grief, I ducked and ran toward the mounted guns, our last line of defence. "How much luma ammo have you got?"

"Not enough," the enforcement officer manning the guns said.

Erebus yelled instructions to the dark djinn, telling them to fall back alongside the Fearless.

"Kenna, you need to get out of here," Irina said. "You need to get back to the fifth dimension. Once this is over, your people will need you. They'll need their queen."

Once this was over. Once the humans were dead, she meant. Like this didn't matter. My eyes pricked. Bella and Mum had given their lives to save mine. Bella had given me her humanity, and Lindrealm was also my home. These were also my people. I would not abandon them.

"Lindrealm needs me right now, Irina." I smiled. "I'm not going anywhere."

"Dammit!" She made an exasperated noise in the back of her throat.

I gripped her upper arm, "But you are. Get back to the fifth dimension. Tell Baal … tell him to take care of the realm for me. To do whatever it takes to protect our people."

Irina pressed her lips together. "I'm not leaving you."

I stood tall, staring down my nose at her. "That wasn't a request. It was an order."

Irina blew out a sharp breath. "Playing the queen card." She shook her head. "Kenna, this is suicide."

I pulled her into a hug. "I'll see you soon." With a final squeeze, I released her and gave her a shove. "Now go!"

She slipped away, probably to Baal's residence where the mirror would lead her home. Erebus and Brett joined me behind the guns.

I turned back to the gate, to the stationary hybrids in Legion's grip. With one word I'd be sealing all our fates.

It was a good word. "Fire!"

Gunfire blazed. The hybrids screamed. Thrashing and bucking. It went on for long minutes, putter, putter, putter. And then it stopped. The bullets were depleted.

The hybrids shook off their injuries, a multitude of eyes staring us down, and then their wounds began to knit.

"Oh, shit."

"They're immune to luma," Brett said.

Like the hybrid scorpions had been immune to my blade. My heart plummeted.

Legion's voice ripped through the silence. "Wrong choice."

The hybrids attacked.

29

The monsters hurtled toward us, and the enforcement officers scattered. Erebus, Brett, and I exchanged glances. The dark djinn and Erebus's clan joined us, slipping behind row of huge guns.

"To the death," Erebus said.

"To the death," his djinn replied.

We were so screwed. My grip on Frieda tightened. If it was time to go down, I'd do it swinging.

And then the sky went dark.

I glanced up to see a multitude of grey shapes … grey beautiful gargoyles. Fargol was here. He'd made it, and he'd brought an army. My pulse lurched and my heart soared. We could do this. Maybe we could do this after all.

And then it began to rain. No, it wasn't rain. It was an emerald haze spraying over the world. It covered the denizens and painted my skin with a jade sheen. Brett bellowed and stumbled back clutching his abdomen. His body began to pulse and shift.

The serum. The gargoyles were deploying the serum. Not in bomb form like we'd planned, but as some kind of mist.

The hybrids began to squeal. They were falling back, rolling onto their sides, shuddering and jerking as the serum stripped away the enhancements Orin's serum had given them. But it didn't stop there. They began to melt into hissing puddles. The serum wasn't just devolving them, it was killing them. Shit. I grabbed Brett and began to drag him out of the blast radius. Too late, yeah, but still maybe if I got him cleaned up …

A gust of air blasted into me and the ground shook.

Fargol landed before me. "Kenna safe."

"Fargol. Help me get him to safety. The serum is killing him."

"No. Serum kill fully evolved denizen hybrid. Not kill human. Not kill Brett."

Oh thank god. I lowered Brett to the ground where he shuddered and curled into a ball. Already the diamond skin was melting away and pink human skin was visible beneath the thin layer of crystal that remained. Hair was sprouting from his newly formed scalp. His face was hidden, but it would be his face. I knew it. My friend was back. But he was in no shape to fight.

The dying wails of the denizens were accompanied by an eerie howl of rage.

Legion.

Fuck you.

"Fargol, get Brett to the palace, get him to Irina. Can you do that for me?"

Fargol looked torn. He glanced over his huge stone shoulder at the denizens in the final throes of an agonising death.

"I'll be fine. I promise."

"Fargol come back."

I threw my arms around him and pressed my cheek to his rocky one. "I love you. Thank you for saving our lives."

His chest rumbled, and then his huge arms closed around me. He held my lightly, careful not to crush. "Fargol love Kenna too. Fargol always save Kenna."

I stepped back and he released me.

"Fargol be back." He scooped up Brett and took to the air, his powerful wings sending gusts of emerald tainted air into my face.

Around me Fearless celebrated with whoops and high fives.

"It doesn't feel over," Erebus said.

He was right. Instead of loosening, the knot in my abdomen tightened. A sense of foreboding tingled up my arm and settled in my brain. There was more.

A radio crackled to life.

"The Twilight Gate is under attack." A tinny voice screamed down the connection. "Send back-up immediately. Figures on horseback, I repeat we are under attack by figures on horseback. They're killing everyone."

This shouldn't be happening. They'd salted the gate, how was The Hunt able to come through? Oh, god. Oh damn. The salt was the wrong kind of salt. It was just sodium chloride, but the salt that kept them at bay in Twilight was born from the tears of the ocean people. It was a different kind of salt, possibly more of a curse or an enchantment.

We had no defence.

The Hunt was here, and we were fucked. There was no stopping that shit. No slowing it down. It would take us all with it. It belonged to Legion, and we'd just pissed it off. There would be no more chances for my people, in Lindrealm or in the fifth dimension. But I had to try.

The remaining Fearless gathered round. I recognised several faces, but many were new—young cadets. Karl stood out as the most seasoned of them.

"Karl, can you man this gate with the Fearless? If any more hybrids come through I'm sure the gargoyles will spray them, but you can handle the regular ones, right?"

"Yeah, we got this."

"Okay, then I'll see you when this is over."

"Brett?" he asked.

"He's safe."

He nodded, his shoulders sagging in relief.

"Come on. Let's move out." I headed toward the Twilight gate, Erebus and dark djinn in tow.

The Twilight gate was a mile off, and we made the journey on foot, alternating between jogs and sprints. My old prosthetic would have given up the ghost by now, but the high-tech one was a machine.

My bionic limb kept me on my feet, even though the rest of my mortal body was flagging. The flame inside was growing in strength though; soon I'd be ready to burn the shit outta the black crap in my veins, but not yet. Right now I needed to keep the flame's power in reserve, just in case.

We approached the bridge to chaos. Bodies ran to and fro, bursting into shadow at the touch of an ethereal whip or the slice of a shadow sword. The Hunt was riding, and the bridge was its domain. The Fearless on the bridge were attempting to fight back using their everlight swords, but all the everlight succeeded in doing was block the blows of The Hunt. It failed to hurt them.

This was futile, I knew it, we all knew it, and yet we descended on that bridge as if we had every chance of prevailing. The Hunt weren't wolves or bears this time. They were five riders in flowing cloaks and deep hoods. They turned on us, whips flailing in the air and swords swishing. An arrow made of ember whizzed by my head.

Fuck!

My hand itched and burned.

It was in my blood calling to me. Come join us, it said. You belong with us.

"Screw you!" I attacked with Frieda, going into ninja mode. No thinking, just instinct.

The nearest rider's horse reared up, neighing in panic, its ember eyes flaring.

"Back the fuck off." I advanced.

Erebus and the dark djinn advanced with me. Like a hungry ink stain, we moved in on the rider.

The horse trotted back, and then the rider yanked on the reins, turning away and galloping down the bridge toward the scattered humans and the Fearless fighting alone.

"Do not fear. Do not run!" A megaphone amplified voice echoed across the bridge.

That voice, I knew that voice. He came into a view a moment later, his tiny robed form waddling toward us, and at his back was a determined mob of people: humans, djinn, Twilighters. They came in force—Father Cimran and his congregation.

What was he doing? "Get back!" I waved my arms in warning. "Get back. You're gonna get killed."

Even at a distance his smile was a dazzling thing. And then it was obscured by the megaphone.

"Together we are strong. They seek to divide and reap. Together we are a power to be reckoned with."

What was he saying? It clicked and settled in my mind. The Hunt reaped. It chased and it isolated, and it fed Legion. It had retreated when I'd advanced with the dark djinn at my back.

Maybe Father Cimran was right.

The congregation was close, only a few metres at our back. I grabbed Erebus's arm. "Together we are stronger."

His eyes narrowed and then he nodded. "Back up. Join the mass."

The congregation began to sing—some hymn I'd heard a long time ago, words I'd thought I'd forgotten. But my lips were moving of their own volition and the heat of a hundred bodies pressed at my back.

We were one.

We were together.

Father Cimran smiled up at me. "Good to see you again Kenna."

"It's good to see you too, you old goat."

The Hunt faltered in its attack. The riders turned their horses this way and that, as if unsure of their next move.

"How did you know what to do?" I asked him.

"I didn't. I just had faith."

The Hunt backed up and we advanced. Slowly, surely, we pushed it toward the gate—a hundred voices rising up in song. In that moment we were a people united regardless of colour, creed, or race. We were one. These were my people. A stream of thought began to unravel in my mind. They were all my people, the humans, the djinn, and the fae, and … Sabriel? What he had done to me … It made sense now.

Adamaris's words made sense, and a pit of sorrow opened up inside me.

I touched Erebus's arm. "I know how to stop it. I know how to stop Legion. I need to go. Now."

His expression hardened. "Then I am coming with you."

"No, you need to—"

He cut me off and turned to Aidan. "Take charge, keep the humans safe."

Aidan grinned. "It is what we do."

I could have protested, could have told Erebus he had to stay, ordered him even—not sure how much good that would have done—but the hidden part of me, the little girl who was afraid of the dark and things that went bump in the night, raised her head. I would be going into the bogeyman's lair, and I didn't want to go alone.

I met Aidan's eye. "Just keep doing this."

He nodded.

My arm tingled.

"Where are we headed?" Erebus asked.

"To the Black Forest. Legion is beneath it."

"How can you know that?"

I held up my hand. "I had a vision."

His mouth tightened. "And what do you intend to do once we get there?"

A shadow flew over us and then Fargol's huge bulk landed before us. An icy gust of air followed, and Baal appeared beside him.

His took in the carnage and then his gaze found me. Relief flashed in his emerald eyes and then I was pressed to his chest, his face buried in my hair.

"Dammit, Kenna. You could have been killed."

"I had to stay."

"I know." He squeezed, and then pulled back. "But we need to get you out of here now. There is nothing more that we can do here. Now that Legion has failed in recruiting soldiers, he will turn his attention to the fifth dimension. He will come at us in force. Your people need you."

"No. They need this to be over. And I know how. We need to get to the Black Forest."

"What's in the Black Forest?" Baal asked.
"I'll tell you when we get there."

<u>30</u>

Baal and I landed on the outskirts of the forest. Now that we were here, it all seemed like a dream—the vision, my revelation, the conviction. But it was our only shot, because Baal was right, Legion would attack the fifth dimension soon. There was no doubt in my mind that he had more hybrids. That he was simply biding his time. He'd forced our hand into using all the luma bullets, so if he sent more airborne hybrids we were screwed. I knew what I had to do, but whether I'd be successful or not was another matter.

"Kenna, why are we here? Speak to me," Baal said. He lifted my chin with the crook of his finger and ran his warm gaze over my face. "Why do I have this terrible feeling in the pit of my stomach?" He pressed his forehead to mine. "Tell me you aren't going to do something incredibly brave but incredibly dangerous."

Oh, god, I loved him so much it hurt. "I can't tell you that."

He kissed me, hard and desperate and punishing. His hands tangled in my hair and fisted almost painfully.

He pulled back. "I cannot lose you."

"You won't." Then why did the words taste like ash?

Fargol landed on the outskirts of the Black Forest. He released Erebus, who stumbled forward, his face pale.

"Well, that was … interesting," Erebus said.

Fargol chuckled. "Erebus not like heights."

"Yes," Erebus said. "Erebus does not like heights." He straightened. "Kenna, you said you knew how to kill Legion?"

"I think. No. I believe I can kill Legion."

Beside me Baal's body went into alert mode, tense and vibrating.

Erebus blinked down at me. "And how will you kill him?"

"Adamaris said that only the harmony of races could destroy Legion. And at first I thought it mean us all working together, and yeah, that kinda worked against The Hunt, but then I realised something else … I realised the harmony of races was inside me."

Erebus stared at me blankly.

Baal exhaled sharply. "You are fae. You are djinn and you are human."

Comprehension dawned in Erebus's pretty eyes.

I nodded. "Yes. But I also have an element of angel in me now … after Sabriel's sacrifice, and Adamaris said I was the last of his bloodline too."

Erebus's eyes lit up in excitement. "Yes. Yes, I think you are right. This could be it. And you know where it resides?"

"There's a tree, a huge tree covered in moss, I think it's the gateway to the abyss."

"Wait," Baal said. "How will you kill it? How do you know that a special weapon of some kind isn't needed?"

"I think I am the weapon."

"And what if you're wrong?"

"Then we get our arses out of there, stat, and think of a plan B."

Fargol led the way, crunching through the bracken and clearing a path with his huge frame. I walked behind him, searching for the damn tree. We'd walked for maybe five minutes when Fargol took a left, cutting between two huge trees. I made to follow and my hand lit up in pain.

"Dammit!" I shook it and took a step back. The pain ebbed.

"Are you all right?" Baal asked.

"Yeah. One sec." I took a step forward and fire lit up my veins. "I think my hand is trying to guide us."

"Okay," Baal said. "Which way?"

"Well, it wants me to find it. It wants me to come to it. So it would warn me if I was going off track, right?"

"That makes sense," Erebus said.

I turned right and took a step. No pain. "This way."

Using the sting, or lack thereof, as I guide, we finally found the tree. It was even larger than I recalled from my vision. Fargol stepped aside and I placed my hand on the mossy bark, searching for that soft entrance. The wood was unyielding, and for a split second I considered the possibility that I'd been wrong, then discarded it. My vision had gotten me this far. My hand sank into the bark.

Bingo.

Ducking down, I pushed through. My boots met stone. It was pitch black in here. Using my hands as guides, I walked forward. It was a tunnel, a downward sloping passageway.

"Fargol is staying behind," Baal said. "He can't fit through the gap. He wanted to make the aperture larger, but I convinced him against that." Baal's breath was warm on the back on my neck. "Wouldn't want to alert Legion of our arrival."

"Oh, I'm entirely sure he knows I'm here."

"Let's just find him and finish this."

We descended further into the tree, into the earth. Dank chill seeped into my bones and then there was light—a sickly green glow. The walls were coated in it—some kind of slime, underground flora, a mould or something.

"Don't touch it," Baal warned. "It looks dangerous."

"It looks gross."

The passage opened up into a chamber with a network of tunnels shooting off it, and I was gripped by déjà vu. It reminded me of the test we'd had to complete at the Academy. We'd been sent into an underground cavern much like this, armed with nothing but the skill passed down and an everlight sword. The objective had been survival.

Much like now.

Except this time I was planning on being the hunter, not the hunted.

"Which way?"

I made a circuit of the chamber, passing each tunnel. Not even a twitch in my hand. "I don't know." I glanced upward and froze. "Um, guys …"

The ceiling was a mass of pulsing egg sacs, they glowed softly and their contents could be seen writhing, pushing, and stretching.

Erebus cursed.

Baal grabbed my hand. "We need to get out of here. Those things are about to—"

Denizens dropped into the chamber, still slimy and wet from their egg sacs. Creatures the likes of nothing I'd ever seen: pincered, and suckered, with way too many appendages to count. There was no time for shock. We countered the attack, ducking and swinging. To my right Baal blasted ice into a denizen's open mouth, freezing the thing solid. I dropped and rolled out of range of a stabbing stinger. Erebus finished that fucker off for me. But they kept coming. Dropping from the ceiling in waves that seemed way too coordinated.

This place was a hive and the influx wouldn't stop. Baal's bellow of pain had me faltering. I leapt back just in time to avoid being a scuttler's dinner, and ran toward Baal. He was on the ground, his arm hanging at an odd angle. Blood was pouring from a wound at his shoulder and another on his head.

His eyes widened. "Watch out!"

I spun, sword sweeping out in an arch and decapitating a creeper. "Shit, shit, shit." I hauled him to his feet, groaning under his weight. "We have to get into the tunnels." I dove for the nearest exit. "Erebus, come on!"

Erebus sliced off the head of what looked like a crawler, and ran toward me. He was barely a foot away when something burst from his chest. The tip of a stinger ... the tip ... oh fuck. Blood sprayed from his mouth and his whole body froze. He blinked as if surprised at this turn of events, and then he focused on me. Our eyes locked, sorrow etched into his face. And then he was yanked backward, back into the chamber with the monsters. They descended on him, covering him with their horrific bodies, and my scream was a monster all of its own.

31

I was being pulled away.

"We need to go. Kenna," Baal said. "There is nothing we can do for him."

Erebus … Erebus was dead. Dead.

My cheek stung and my eyes watered.

Baal stared at me, bleary eyed, swaying on his feet. "I'm sorry. I had to snap you out of it."

"You hit me." I touched my cheek.

"We have to go." He fell back against the tunnel wall. "I don't know how much longer I can stay with you."

The haze over my mind dissipated. I'd lost my sister, my mum, and now Erebus; there was no way I was losing Baal. But he was bleeding out. Ripping off my shirt, I quickly tied it around the wound in his shoulder. Something had taken a chunk out of his arm. He was pale, shaking, and would probably go into shock soon.

"Why aren't you healing?"

"I don't know."

Allowing him to use me as a crutch, I ventured further into the tunnel, leaving the screams and screeches of the chamber behind. Leaving Erebus behind.

The tears were hot on my cheeks and I let them fall. Legion would pay for this, for everything it had done.

The tunnel opened up further and a strange melodic humming drifted to my ears.

"What is that?" Baal asked.

"I don't know."

But we found out a moment later as we took a curve in the tunnel and came upon a wretched figure chained to the wall. It was female in rags, her hair long and tangled, her face almost skeletal, but her eyes were bright and intelligent. She cut off her song when she caught sight of us.

"Marigold?" she cocked her head. "What? No. You can't be here!" She squinted and stared at me for a long beat. "You're not my daughter."

Oh god ... Was this Orin's wife? My grandmother? Mum and I had been right to assume that Legion had taken her. He'd held her here as leverage over Orin to prevent the king from breaking its hold on his mind. He'd used what Orin loved the most and held it hostage. What had he promised the king? What lengths would Orin have gone for love?

"I'm Kenna, Marigolds daughter."

She closed her eyes and nodded, a deep sigh rattled her chest. "Yes. Better that you do it."

"Me?"

"Yes, my sweet child. You must set me free."

Of course. Shit. "Baal, can you stand?"

He nodded.

I slipped out from under his arm and drew Frieda. "Just stay still while I cut the chains."

She cocked her head and smiled. "No, dear. You need to kill me."

She said it matter of fact and completely calm.

"And do it fast." She frowned. "Orin is mounting his horse. He is about to lead his army to battle. He is fighting, but with half a heart. My husband is a strong man. He will survive my loss, and his anger will free him. Once I am gone, he will no longer be chained."

"Do it," Baal said. "If killing her can stop Orin, then you must do it."

It was the only way, and yet I couldn't stop my hands shaking. "There must be another way. Maybe if we freed you and took you to him?"

"There is no time. Once he rides he will be consumed. Orin will be lost to Legion, and his army will follow the horror that fell to this world. Please, Kenna. Let me be free. By killing me you set us all free." A single tear tracked down her cheek.

I gripped Frieda's handle tight and plunged it into my grandmother's heart.

"Oh …" Her smile was filled with wonder, and then the light in her eyes died.

The ground shook and a roar reverberated around us. My hand lit up with pain, but not as a warning, as punishment for what I'd done. I could sense Legion's intention. His rage. And I was coming for him.

Slipping my shoulder under Baal's arm, I led us down the tunnel. He was close. So close now. The next turn brought us to a stone stairway leading down. Baal's weight grew with each step. He was waning. I needed to get him out of here or he might not make it. There must have been something in the creature's saliva, some kind of anti-clotting agent. I paused and looked back.

"No," Baal said. "We go on and we do this. We end this. Orin may have broken Legion's hold, and maybe not, maybe he was too far gone. We can't take the risk." He reached up to caress my face. "The fifth dimension is our home. Our people are depending on us." He looked deep into my eyes. "This is our chance to end this."

The stairs spat us out into a cavern, and in its centre was a huge black blob. It pulsed slowly like a heartbeat. This was Legion—this heinous mass with no real form of its own. It was an infection, its black tendrils burrowed into the earth, into the rock.

Baal entered the cavern behind me and grabbed the stone wall to steady himself. I wiped the blood from my face and raised my everlight sword.

Laughter echoed around the chamber. Legion's laughter.

"What do you intend to do with that?" Legion said.

I glanced at Baal but he looked unfazed.

"Did you hear that?"

"What?"

"You didn't?"

So it was in my head. Communicating via its taint in my veins no doubt. But that was about to end. I stepped up to the disgusting mass and plunged my sword deep. The thing's hide was tough, had to give it that, but once Frieda got past that, the inside was like butter.

Legion laughed.

I stabbed again and again, my blood boiling with impotence.

"Kenna, it's not working." Baal said. He coughed—a wet bloody sound. "We need to get out of here."

He was right, this wasn't working. It made no sense. I was the harmony of races. I was sure of it. I was the weapon. Then why, slash, wasn't, slice, this working?

"My turn," Legion said.

Black tendrils shot out of the mass and grabbed me.

"Kenna!"

Baal ran toward me, but a thick black limb smashed into him, sweeping him back and slamming him against the rock wall.

"Kenna, no!"

We locked gazes as Legion's grip tightened, ready to take me. "I love you. I love you so much."

And then I was yanked down.

Down into Legion.

***

It was inside me again. Filling me up anew, crawling up my spine. I had to fight. Had to unleash the flame. I summoned it now and it flared, ripping through the darkness, cleansing me, forcing Legion to loosen its grip, but before I could break free Legion infected me again. Once again, my luma-laced fire burned through the infection, and once again he tainted me.

There was barely a flicker left inside me, not enough to burn the crap from my veins. I was empty, a shell for Legion.

"Submit." His voice was a caress. "Submit and be free."

But it wasn't freedom he offered. It was servitude. Like Orin, like The Hunt. Like anyone he'd ever tainted. I was moving, down, down into the abyss. The walls were pulsing crimson, flesh and blood. I was descending into hell, but I wouldn't go without a fight. Clawing and kicking I slowed my downward motion.

"Now you will see my true heart, and once you see it, it cannot be unseen. You will belong to me."

I froze mid kick. His true heart?

A heart was vulnerable, the pump that kept the machine running.

"Submit and enter my heart."

I was fucked either way, but there still might be a chance for everyone else. I tested the tiny flickering flame inside me, nothing more than the light on the head of a match. But it was my last hope. Closing my eyes, I let go. Allowed myself to be swept down into the bowels of the earth, to sink into Legion's core, it's pulsing warm heart. Hands reached for me, rubbing eagerly, mouths latched onto me, sucking wantonly. Don't move, don't expend any energy. Because this was it, my final moment, my final act. It would be everything or it would be nothing. Either way, it was curtains for me. Bella's face swam behind my closed lids. Her sunny smile and crazy laugh, the scent of Mum's freshly baked scones. Baal's indigo hair between my fingers, his lips on mine, his emerald gaze warm on my face.

So many lives.

I'd lived enough, and yet I wanted, desperately with all my heart, to live one more lifetime with him.

The fingers on my flesh turned to claws, the mouths sprouted teeth. Pain ripped through me and the flame flickered.

Not yet, just a moment longer.

The heart would consume me now. Tear me to shreds, the inevitable action was locked into a single moment of tension as the teeth and the claws paused, as if to gather their strength.

This was it.

My end.

But by god I was gonna take this fucker with me.

The tension snapped, the claws tore and the teeth gnashed. My scream was white hot lightening, and as I came undone, the tiny flame inside me was set free.

Free.

Burn baby, fucking burn.

<u>32</u>

Was this death? Was I dead? It was dark, so dark. Was this the afterlife? What about Bella? Did I get to be with her, and Mum … I wanted to be with Mum.

The darkness began to fill with light, and the silhouette of a figure appeared.

"Kenna?"

"Sabriel? Is that you? I thought you were dead."

He laughed softly. "Nothing really ever dies."

"Legion. Please tell me he's dead at least."

"No, Kenna. But he is gone from our world. Your sacrifice was the sacrifice of all the races. It had a power of its own, one greater than destruction and fear and chaos."

"Good. I'm glad. So what now?"

"I'm here to take you home."

"Home? As in heaven?"

"No, Kenna, not yet. Not for a long time."

What was he saying?

His hand slipped into mine. "Are you ready?"

Pulse pounding in my throat, I stepped into the light.

EPILOGUE

My new coronation gown felt twice as heavy as it had that morning. The tailor had made me a replica to replace the one ruined when I'd been kidnapped. All the beading and the tiny gems sewn into it had doubled in weight throughout the day. I stood before the full-length mirror pulling pins from my hair. Man it felt good to let it down. My crown sat on my dresser, another bulky item that would need to be downsized. Kicking off my shoes, I padded onto the balcony and tipped my face up to the night sky.

This was real.

I was alive.

My people were safe.

I reminded myself of it daily. Brett was back in Lindrealm heading up the Fearless division, although since the hoard had settled, denizen activity had calmed down and Lindrealm was enjoying a spate of relative peace. It would stay this way. I'd make sure of it.

Lauren was managing things for me in Twilight as Regent in my absence, and the black mages were helping settle the city. There would be a meeting soon, with Dawn and Dusk to hash out new treaties and build a new future. Oh, and another coronation, because, yep, I was now the queen of Twilight too—no idea how I was going manage two realms, but I wasn't lacking in support.

A soft knock at the door caught my attention. "Come in," I called over my shoulder.

I didn't need to turn around, didn't need a tether to tell me that Erebus had entered the room. The air crackled with energy. The power that he'd expended all these years to create his clan was now nestled back where it belonged, inside him. When he'd almost died, they'd come to him—Vale, Baron, and Aidan. They'd sacrificed their autonomy, their very selves to save his life, melding with him and going home. Erebus had been restored to what he'd always been, the most powerful dark djinn in his tribe, the reason The Hunt had been unable to take him. He was something else, something new, and it was almost too painful to look at him now.

"Kenna, I wanted to say goodbye."

My chest tightened. "I don't know if I'm ready."

"Yes. You are. You will make a fine queen. You were given a second chance, just like I was. You are whole again. Just as I am. We both have a purpose. I just need to find mine."

I glanced down at my legs, obscured by the gown. The urge to lift it and check was almost too much, but I knew what I would see. Two flesh and bone legs. I'd come back, and I'd come back whole.

I turned my head to look at him, blinking at the sheen to his skin and the stars in his eyes. He was painfully, savagely beautiful. "Where will you go?"

"I do not know. But we are a nomadic people. Travel is in our blood."

"Will you come back?" Why was I crying?

He reached up and wiped away my tears. "I do not know."

I nodded. "I'll miss you."

"And I you." He moved closer and pressed a kiss to my forehead. "Another time and another place, Kenna …"

I locked gazes with him, my vision blurring. "Another time and another place."

He stepped back. "Goodbye, Kenna."

He vanished in a puff of black smoke.

I sagged against the balcony railing, puffed out my cheeks and blew out a breath. Get it together, you have a rendezvous to go to, and as if on cue the beat of Fargol's wings filled the air. He landed lightly on the balcony and inclined his head.

"Your majesty."

"Fargol …" My tone had warning.

He grinned. "Fine, Fargol call you Kenna."

"Do that."

"Kenna ready?" He held out his hands.

"Yes." I walked up to him and allowed him to wrap his fingers around my waist. "Let's go."

Fargol took to the air, taking me with him. The balcony slipped away, and the palace grounds came into view, kissed by moonlight. I closed my eyes and breathed in the night scents of jasmine, honeysuckle, and stardust.

And then we were descending. Soft grass tickled my toes and Fargol's fingers slipped from my waist. He didn't land, but rose back up into the air and away. I stood in the centre of the secret garden, hands clasped before me, heart pounding in my chest. The scent of liquorice filled the air and my pulse jumped in my throat. Baal had promised me a midnight picnic, and I was starving, but not for food.

He hadn't touched me since I'd been resurrected. He'd treated me like I was made of china, as if I'd shatter with the breeze. Weeks had passed and I'd longed for his touch, to feel him inside me, his heart beating against mine. I was done waiting.

He stepped out from the shadows and walked toward me. His indigo hair was tousled, his shirt was unbuttoned, exposing his smooth tanned chest, and there was a hungry gleam in his eyes. It set my already erratic pulse galloping.

"When you died, a part of me died with you," he said. "The past few weeks I've been waiting to wake up, thinking this was just a dream, that maybe we both died in that place, that Fargol hadn't brought the black mages to save us. You die in my arms every night, and every day I watch you, thinking you are a dream."

"I'm not a dream. I'm here."

"I know, my heart knows," he stepped closer, the heat of his body pressing against me. "My body knows." His voice was a low rumble of need. "I'm not waiting any longer."

Oh thank god.

He gently gripped my chin and ran his thumb over my bottom lip, eliciting a moan. "Do you remember my promise?" The fingers of his free hand trailed across the bodice of my gown, teasing the tops of my breasts.

"The coronation gown," my voice was breathless, my core liquid.

His smile was a slow burn of delicious intent. "I always keep my word."

Yeah, best day ever.

THE END

If you enjoyed Kenna's story, make sure to check out the other books by Debbie Cassidy for your next obsession.

The Gatekeeper Chronicles
Marked by Sin
Hunted by Sin
Claimed by Sin

The Witch Blood Chronicles
(Spin off to the Gatekeeper Chronicles but can be read independently)
Binding Magick
Defying Magick
Embracing Magick
Unleashing Magick

The Sleeping Gods Series
Forest of Demons
Desert of Destiny

The Shadowlands Series
Written as Amos Cassidy
Shadow Reaper
Shadow Eater
Shadow Destiny

About the Author

Debbie Cassidy lives in England, Bedfordshire, with her three kids and very supportive husband. Coffee and chocolate biscuits are her writing fuels of choice, and she is still working on getting that perfect tower of solitude built in her back garden. Obsessed with building new worlds and reading about them, she spends her spare time daydreaming and conversing with the characters in her head—in a totally non-psychotic way of course. She writes High Fantasy, Urban Fantasy, and Science Fiction. Debbie also writes dark, diverse Urban Fantasy fiction under the pen name Amos Cassidy, with her best friend Richard Amos. Connect with Debbie via her website at debbiecassidyauthor.com or twitter @authordcassidy. Sign up for her NEWSLETTER to stay informed of upcoming releases.

Made in the USA
Coppell, TX
28 January 2022